**She'd Seen Enough Pictures
To Know Rafe Carlisle Was
The Middle Son Of One Of
Australia's Richest And
Most Newsworthy Families.**

He might hold some fancy executive title in the family's hotel group, but from what she'd read, Rafe Carlisle didn't get too close to anything resembling work. Play was more his thing—playing in nightclubs, playing in casinos, playing with women.

And wasn't that just her luck? One of the notoriously rich and handsome "Princes of the Outback" drops out of the sky into her paddock, and it has to be the glamor boy!

"And you are?" he asked faintly.

"Catriona McConnell." *Impoverished, non-newsworthy, hardworking pastoralist, with not a drop of blue blood.*

Except what did it matter which Carlisle had landed in her paddock? He wasn't the answer to her prayers.

He was simply a stranger—albeit a rich stranger—in need of *her* help.

Dear Reader

Silhouette Desire has a fantastic selection of novels for you this month, starting with our latest DYNASTIES: THE ASHTONS title, *Condition of Marriage* by Emilie Rose. Pregnant by one man…married to another, sounds like another Ashton scandal to me! *USA TODAY* bestselling author Peggy Moreland is back with a brand-new TANNERS OF TEXAS story. In *Tanner Ties,* it's a female Tanner who is looking for answers…and finds romance instead.

Our TEXAS CATTLEMAN'S CLUB: THE SECRET DIARY also continues this month with Brenda Jackson's fabulous *Strictly Confidential Attraction,* the story of a shy secretary who gets the chance to play house with her supersexy boss. Sheri WhiteFeather returns with another sexy Native American hero. You fell for Kyle in Sheri's previous Silhouette Bombshell novel, but just wait until you get to really know him in *Apache Nights.*

Two compelling miniseries also continue this month: Linda Conrad's *Reflected Pleasures,* the second book in THE GYPSY INHERITANCE—a family with a legacy full of surprises. And Bronwyn Jameson's PRINCES OF THE OUTBACK series has its second installment with *The Rich Stranger*—a man who must produce an heir in order to maintain his fortune.

Here's hoping this September's selections give you all the romance, all the drama and all the sensationalism you've come to expect from Silhouette Desire.

Melissa Jeglinski

Melissa Jeglinski
Senior Editor
Silhouette Desire

Please address questions and book requests to:
Silhouette Reader Service
U.S.: 3010 Walden Ave., P.O. Box 1325, Buffalo, NY 14269
Canadian: P.O. Box 609, Fort Erie, Ont. L2A 5X3

THE RICH STRANGER

BRONWYN JAMESON

Published by Silhouette Books

America's Publisher of Contemporary Romance

This one is dedicated to all the friends I've made
through the eHarlequin community, especially the
Brainstorming Desireables, the Aussie Hour chatters
and the wonderful hosties. Thank you for the support,
the feedback, the laughter and for bringing
the whole world to my little corner.

SILHOUETTE BOOKS

ISBN 0-373-76680-7

THE RICH STRANGER

Visit Silhouette Books at www.eHarlequin.com

Printed in U.S.A.

BRONWYN JAMESON

spent much of her childhood with her head buried in a book. As a teenager, she discovered romance novels, and it was only a matter of time before she turned her love of reading them into a love of writing them. Bronwyn shares an idyllic piece of the Australian farming heartland with her husband and three sons, a thousand sheep, a dozen horses, assorted wildlife and one kelpie dog. She still chooses to spend her limited downtime with a good book. Bronwyn loves to hear from readers. Write to her at bronwyn@bronwynjameson.com.

OUTBACK GLOSSARY

Akubra—popular brand of stockman's hat

Bloke—man, guy

Bourke—town in the northwest of New South Wales

Circular Quay—busy ferry quay and station near Sydney Harbour Bridge

Cooee—a loud call meant to travel a long distance. Hence, *within cooee* means nearby; *not with cooee* means a long way away.

Coolabah—trees made famous through the song "Waltzing Matilda"

Corker—noun meaning an excellent, great, wonderful thing

Crikey—expression of surprise or amazement

Kelpie—breed of sheepdog

Paddock—field

Pastoralist—rancher

Ripper—great, fantastic

Station—large outback property comparable to an American ranch

Steers—castrated male cattle

Utility truck (ute)—pickup truck

One

No new mail.

Catriona McConnell stared at the message on her computer screen, not surprised, not even disappointed so much as numb. She resisted the urge to hit the Receive Mail button again, just in case her e-mail program magically retrieved the message she needed to see—the one it hadn't found on the last three attempts—from somewhere deep inside the bowels of the World Wide Web. But Drew hadn't responded to any of the messages she'd left over the past week, via every contact point she could dig up, so why would he respond to her latest desperate e-mail?

Because he's your friend, your one-time lover. He grew up next door. He should care.

"Because neighbors care? Yeah, right!"

No longer numb, Cat turned off the computer and shoved her chair back from the time-battered table she called a desk.

A churning mix of anger and disillusionment and what-the-blazes-will-I-do-now anxiety roared low in her ears, in perfect pitch with the rumble of distant thunder.

Halfway to the door she paused, listening as the noise gathered enough strength to vibrate through the roof and into the solid mud-brick walls. Not despair, not thunder ahead of the forecast evening storms, but the roar of a plane. A plane flying so low over Cat's Australian outback homestead that she instinctively ducked.

Then she got moving.

Before the screen door had slapped shut in her wake, she'd hurdled the veranda rail onto the lawn…or the semidead patch of grass that used to be lawn. Eyes peeled upward, she whipped around in a half circle until she found the plane, a bright slash of white against the darkening sky.

Drew?

Heart pounding with recharged hope, she followed the low dip of one wing as the aircraft banked off to the west. And wouldn't that be just like him? Ignore her flurry of messages, give no advance warning, go for the big dramatic entrance. She guessed he'd deliberately buzzed her home and now he would swoop off to land at his father's airstrip, ten miles to the northwest.

Cat started for her truck without thinking, then drew up short. She didn't want to visit with Gordon Samuels, the snake, but if the unexpected fly-in visitor *was* Drew, she needed to be there. She needed to know what the hell had gone down between father and son regarding the money she'd borrowed.

The whole future of Corroboree, the station that had been in the McConnell family for six generations, depended on the answer. Her whole future depended on the answer. And the way she felt about Drew Samuels right now, *his* life might also depend upon it!

Jamming her stockman's hat low on her forehead, Cat stalked the last yards to her Landcruiser. But before opening

the door, she glanced skyward again, and her heart jumped
and jammed in her throat. The plane hadn't banked to fly
northwest. It had turned a full 180 degrees and now hung low
against the horizon, an insignificant-looking dot against the
angry billow of storm clouds.

"Oh, no," she breathed. Chill apprehension shivered
through her bones. "You aren't. You wouldn't."

Drew knew the locale too well to attempt a landing on her
ungraded, out-of-use, pathetic excuse for an airstrip. Surely
her last message hadn't sounded so desperate that he'd pull
such a crazy stunt. Heart in mouth she watched the plane dip
out of sight behind a stand of coolabah trees, and that jolted
her out of immobility and into her truck.

All the way to the strip her pulse pounded in rhythm with
the *please no, please no* chant running through her mind. She'd
wished Drew to damnation many times these past months, but
never literally. Her hands clasped the wheel tightly, holding her
speeding vehicle steady against the rutted track and the buf-
feting crosswind. The storm was coming in much faster than
anticipated and it was turning into a real howler.

Almost airborne, her ancient utility truck crested the last
rise and landed with a bone-jarring racket of overstretched
shocks. Cat paid no heed. Her eyes were fixed on the flat
stretch of land ahead and the plane that was shuddering to a
drunken listing stop at one end.

She expelled a long gust of backed-up breath. Not only her
lungs and chest but her whole body ached with a tension that
only eased marginally on seeing the safely grounded plane.
Yup, it had landed safely, but no doubt roughly and bouncily.

And that pretty much described the state of her outback station these days—rough, bouncy but still hanging together in
one piece.

Less than thirty seconds later she wheeled to a halt beneath
the stricken Cessna's wing. Up close she could see the buck-
led landing gear, which listed the whole craft in a pained for-

ward slump. There was no sign of movement, just an ominous stillness.

As she flung her door open, the wind grabbed hold, yanking it from her hand and slamming it back on its hinges. A bolt of lightning cut a jagged path between sky and earth. Thunder boomed loud on its heels.

Cat grimaced as she clambered up to reach the pilot's door. "Please, don't rain yet. Just give me a few minutes." Both her plea to the heavens and her favorite Akubra were wrenched away by the wind's fury, but her aggravation at losing the hat faded when she opened that door.

The plane's sole occupant sat slumped against his restraining seat belt, motionless. A shock of dark hair fell over his forehead, obscuring his eyes but not the bottom half of his face. Cat stared in bewilderment.

She'd been so fixed on Drew that she hadn't considered finding someone else strapped in the pilot's seat. An olive-skinned someone else with a wide mouth and a sulky fullness to his bottom lip. A stranger, yet Cat felt a vague frisson of recognition as she stared at his dark-whiskered jaw and his strong, squared-off chin.

Another sharp crack of thunder rattled the plane, and Cat shook herself into action. With a firm hand on each shoulder she managed to push his upper body into a more upright position, but he remained out of it.

"You must have conked your head good and hard," she murmured as she removed the radio headset and threaded his hair back behind his ears. His skin, she noticed, was a reassuringly warm contrast to the cool silk of his hair. Gently she probed his head, checked his ears, and found no sign of blood. Reassured, she moved quickly, checking the rest of his body for any sign of broken bones or misaligned joints, for any reaction that might indicate serious injury.

Satisfied he was all in one piece, she rocked back on her heels. Quick-decision time.

Medical help was close to two hours away and if this storm delivered on the fury it promised, the dirt roads might become impassable. Better to get him out of here while she could, get a start toward the hospital, rather than wait around for an ambulance that might not arrive. Moving his large, unconscious form could prove tricky, however, and she lived alone. She ran Corroboree on her own. Calling for a neighbor's help would waste more valuable time.

"Just as well I'm the strapping type," Cat said, mimicking one of her stepmother's kinder descriptions of her sturdy five-foot-eight frame. She preferred to think of herself as a woman equal to the task…whatever that task may be.

She put her hands on her current task's jean-clad knees and shook him gently. When there was no reaction, she took his shoulders in a firmer grip and tried again. "Time to wake up, Sleeping Beauty."

She didn't think that was overstating the facts. His face was a real treat, that mouth nothing short of spectacular. For one crazy second the waking-Sleeping-Beauty scenario flickered through her mind and she considered leaning forward and laying her lips against that beautiful mouth.

Of course she didn't, and not only because, as a rule, she didn't kiss strangers. Even those who looked like Mediterranean gods fallen from the sky. She didn't because his lips started to move, to fashion speech…or at least some unintelligible slurred version of that faculty.

Cat's gaze flew up to meet a pair of surprisingly lucid blue-green eyes, and her pulse began to skitter and race like a startled steer. Because he'd jolted her with his sudden consciousness. Because of all the adrenaline still zapping through her blood from the rush to the strip, from the fear of disaster and the shock of discovery.

And, okay, because he'd come to while she was staring at his mouth and wondering if he would taste as good as he looked.

Then those eyes she'd thought so clear a second before lost focus and glazed over. His complexion looked more wan, almost gray. "Are you okay?" she asked.

He started to nod, then winced as if the movement jarred.

"Head hurts a little, huh?"

"A lot."

"Ah, real words." Cat smiled reassuringly. "Now we've got the tongue figured out, let's see what else we can get working."

Something flickered in those hazy eyes. Humor? Cat rejected the notion. He was not up to wordplay. It was more likely pain.

"I hate to rush you, but I'm afraid we're staring down the barrel of a ripper storm." She reached for the latch on his seat belt. "Ready to rock and roll?"

He winced again, perhaps at the mention of the storm that had no doubt led to his unexpected landing. Perhaps at the prospect of doing anything that involved rocking or rolling. Or perhaps because she wasn't watching what she was doing down there with the seat belt. Her elbows nudged the muscular thighs spread slightly on the seat, her knuckles grazed the hard plane of his abdomen, and suddenly she was all fumbling thumbs until, finally, the catch gave.

Swallowing hard, she got her hands out of harm's way as he started to maneuver himself out of his seat. And, ah, hell, even stooped over she could see that he was taller than she'd imagined, and she didn't know how she would manage getting him down to the ground if—

"Are your legs going to hold you?" she fretted out loud.

Slowly he lifted his head and looked into her eyes. A pained attempt at a smile quirked one corner of his mouth. "Woan collapse on you, babe. Unless you wan' me—"

His slurred voice trailed off, his eyes glazed over, and Cat shook her head. The man could barely stand up and he was flirting? *Give me strength!*

"Okay, hotshot." She reached for his arm. "Let me help."

"I'm okay." He rallied to grip both sides of the doorway. Then he squinted at the view beyond her shoulder. "You're gonna get wet."

Inevitably, since the first fat drops of rain were already soaking into the back of her shirt, but she didn't want to hustle him into slipping and falling. "I'm parked right here, see? Not far to walk in the rain."

Despite her worry, he descended without incident…until his boots hit mother earth and he tilted at the exact same angle as his Cessna. Lightning fast, Cat ducked her shoulder under his arm, taking most of his weight.

"I've got you." She braced her legs when they both threatened to overbalance, and wrapped both arms solidly around his chest.

"Sorry." His mumbled apology was almost lost in an explosion of thunder. "Woozy."

With her face shmooshed up against his ribs, she could hear the solid thud of his heartbeat and feel the vibrant heat of his body right through his butter-soft suede jacket. And with every breath her lungs filled with the scent of hot skin and, well, hot man.

Yup, woozy about summed it up for her, too.

Thankfully, he regained his balance as quickly as before, easing the pressure on her shoulder. Together they shuffled to her truck, and he eased himself gingerly into the passenger seat. Cat had to work to extricate her arm from under his and then, as she dashed around to the driver's side, she filled her lungs with cool, rain-wet air and cleared her head of that giddy reaction.

By the time she'd waited the obligatory tick-tick-tick to warm the diesel engine, the rain was bucketing down. "Lucky," she said, turning to check her passenger as she found first gear and the truck lurched into motion. "We'd have been drenched in no time."

His head was back, propped against the top of the seat, but slowly it rolled toward her. His eyes opened and focused with some effort on her face. "Rafe…Car…lisle."

For a second Cat gazed back into his eyes—she'd never seen the Mediterranean, but her imagination painted it that exact sea-green hue—before it struck her that he was introducing himself. Her heart stuttered a half beat. Of course. That's why she'd felt that niggle of recognition.

No, she hadn't met him, but she'd seen enough pictures plastered through the media to know exactly who Rafe Carlisle was. Middle son of one of Australia's richest and most newsworthy families. The media loved to refer to the Carlisles as Australia's "outback royalty" since they owned so much of the northern cattle country, as well as hotels and property and God knows what else.

But this particular Carlisle brother didn't get his Gucci footwear dirty in outback dust or cattle pats. Rafe Carlisle might hold some fancy executive title in the family's hotel group, but from what she'd read he didn't get too close to anything resembling work. Play was more his thing—playing in nightclubs, playing in casinos, playing with women.

And wasn't that just a measure of the way her luck was hanging? One of the notoriously rich and handsome "princes of the outback" drops out of the sky into her paddock, and it has to be the lightweight glamour boy!

"And you are?" he asked faintly, obviously wanting her side of the introduction.

"Catriona McConnell." *Impoverished, nonnewsworthy, hardworking pastoralist, with not a drop of blue blood to bless myself.*

Except what did it matter which Carlisle had landed in her paddock? He wasn't the answer to her barrage of messages or to her prayers. He wasn't Drew Samuels. He was simply a stranger—albeit a rich stranger—in need of her help. She had to get him medical attention, which meant getting through this deluge to the sealed road before the red dirt track bogged.

She *would* make it unless…

Hardly daring to look, she squinted at the fuel gauge and swore silently at the inaccurate flicker of the needle. How much was in the tank? When had she last filled up? She'd been budgeting, rationing, and she prayed fervently that this latest cutback wasn't about to bite her on the backside.

Rafe woke with a start, dazed and disoriented for the seconds it took to register his surroundings and the woman shaking him by the shoulders. Slowly the pieces came back to him, a series of snapshots that blurred in and out of focus.

He remembered landing the company jet at Bourke Airport, remembered heading out again in the Cessna. The storm he'd thought he could outrace. A hazel-eyed angel of mercy and rain so loud he'd thought it was pounding holes in his skull.

Vaguely he recalled waking at his angel's homestead and the struggle to get him inside. Less vaguely he recalled the cold compress she applied to the side of his head. Such a promising start, spoiled when she insisted he sit still, stay awake and answer the same questions over and over with a persistency that hammered worse than his killer headache.

Realizing she'd succeeded in waking him, Nurse Naggard stopped the shaking and leaned back out of his face. This brought her into clearer focus, and Rafe blinked with surprise. "You showered."

"Only because you kept nagging," she said archly.

He kept nagging? That was rich!

He thought about telling her so, but she shifted again, totally distracting him with the sharp, sweet scent of whatever she'd showered with. And her hair…he hadn't noticed she had so much of it. The mass of damp, brown curls hung almost to her waist. Pity about the twin furrows of worry and annoyance between her brows—they completely ruined the pretty effect.

Rafe started to shake his head with regret, then stopped himself. Any movement caused a rolling wave of nausea, as if his brain hadn't regained its balance after whatever walloping it had taken. She'd told him he'd been out cold for a minute or two, that he must have hit his head during what had been a rough landing.

He didn't remember.

He did remember she'd been wet, right through. Now she wore a green sweater that looked soft and pretty and dry. "You changed," he said. "Good."

"You slept," she countered. "Bad."

Ah, yes, his nagging angel of mercy had a quick mouth. He remembered that now. "I was just resting my eyes."

A lie, but a fair one, given the way she kept trying to blind him. Right on cue she picked up a flashlight and tapped it against the palm of her hand. Her very own instrument of torture.

"No." He held up a hand, keeping her at bay. "Enough is enough. I remember where I am and who I am. I remember my mother's name, my brothers' names, and even my third cousin Jasper's middle name."

The last was an exaggeration, but he'd had it with this routine. Every half hour, her same questions, his same answers, while the beam of light burned a hole clear through his pupil and into his brain.

"Don't be a baby." She picked up his hand and turned it over. Despite the "baby" barb, Rafe let her take his pulse. He liked the cool press of her fingers against his wrist, liked the serious intensity on her face and the infinitesimal movement of her lips as she counted the beats. "Only one more hour, as per the doctor's instructions."

The doctor she'd called when the weather defeated her aim of driving him to the nearest hospital. The instructions involved basic observations and this neuro-responsive BS that he'd endured for at least three hours. And that, he decided, was long enough.

"My pupils are equal and reacting?" he asked.

"Last time I checked, yes, but—"

"Has anything changed in the last half hour?"

"No, but—"

"Fine." Rafe wrested the flashlight from her hand. "No more. I'm going to sleep."

He started to lift his legs, angling himself to lie down, and her voice rose in alarm. "You're not sleeping here. The couch is too short. It's not comfort—"

"It's horizontal." And at the moment that's all Rafe required. To shut his eyes, to stop talking and rest his aching brain—

"There's a bed made up," she relented with a heavy sigh. "But first, are you sure you don't need to call anyone?"

He'd radioed when the storm came up, signaling his intention to land and his location, and she'd since notified authorities. That would suffice for tonight. If he let one of his family members know, he'd end up having to field a barrage of concerned calls. His mother, his big brother, his little brother. His personal assistant. His neighbor. His housekeeper.

What they didn't know wouldn't hurt them. Trying to explain would hurt him. "No calls," he said.

"What about food?"

"Just bed."

He got to his feet. And when his brain took a moment to adjust to the new upright perspective, she helped him steady. He didn't mind the solicitous hand at his elbow, and he liked the sweep of her hair against his shoulder and the scent—peaches, he decided—that drifted from her skin. He enjoyed the brush of her hip against his thigh as she ushered him to a hallway off the living room. And when he started to turn into the first doorway, when she stood her ground and blocked his progress, he *really* enjoyed the soft pressure of her breast against his ribs.

"That's my room," she said, a bit breathless as if she, too, was aware of that unplanned contact. "You're next on the right." She steered him that way. "And it would ease my mind if you could stay awake ten minutes so I can do one more check."

"I'll be asleep in five."

She made an impatient sound, tongue against teeth. "Are you always this difficult?"

"Are you?"

Surprise swung her gaze up to meet his. A pretty mix of gray and green and brown, her eyes, in the muted light of the hallway. "I'm not difficult."

"Huh." Whirring head notwithstanding, he felt an urge to tease—to look into those pretty eyes and ask if that meant she was easy. But she nudged the door to his room open, flicked the light switch, and the sudden brightness knifed through his brain.

A short uncensored curse hissed from his mouth. Muttering a quick apology, she turned the light off, but Rafe had caught a glimpse of the bed. Big, broad, dressed in a mile-thick quilt, it crooned, *Come to Mama.*

"Oh, yeah," Rafe murmured, pushing off the doorjamb to answer that sultry siren's call.

Catriona, apparently, moved too.

Perhaps she thought he needed help negotiating the semi-darkness. Perhaps she was still hand-on-elbow in case her patient fell. Whatever the reason, she was there at his side, fussing about extra blankets and bathroom directions, when he made it bedside.

And when, with a blissful moan, he collapsed into the thick folds of feather-down comforter, she overbalanced and went down with him. He heard the heavy hitch of her surprised breath as the bed came up to greet their fall. Horizontal at last, engulfed in sweet-smelling quilt and sweeter-smelling female, Rafe couldn't bring himself to move.

He should, he mused, at least move his hand—the one resting atop a very sweet curve of breast. And he would, just as soon as he summoned enough energy. Meanwhile his eyes drifted shut and the night he'd planned before leaving Sydney drifted through his dwindling consciousness.

If not for the storm he'd be at his destination now. His unexpected arrival would have shocked the blazes out of his one-time girlfriend, Nikki Bates, but not nearly as much as the reason for his visit. Right about now he'd have been getting to that point. Despite a mountain of reservations and providing he could wring the words from his resistive mind, he'd have been asking Nikki how she felt about having his baby.

Two

Cat woke in her own bed, lost for several seconds in the realm where dream and reality collided. It all came back to her then, and she sat up in a rush of shed bedclothes and remembered anxiety.

Rafe Carlisle. Concussed. In her guest room.

She'd last checked on him—she glanced at her watch and sucked in a quick breath—more than five hours ago. Blast. She hadn't expected to sleep so soundly. She hadn't expected to sleep much at all.

Concern sent her scurrying from her room. Caution sent her back to grab her robe, which she pulled on and secured with a double knot as she paused to listen at his door. The silence was rendered oddly loud by the thick thud of her own heartbeat. She tapped lightly on the door, tucked a mass of sleep-tangled hair behind her ear and pressed that ear flush against the timber.

Not a sound.

Quietly she pushed the door open and realized she'd been holding her breath when it rushed from her lungs in a whoosh. Relief, she told herself, since he was still in bed, asleep, not standing there in some state of undress.

And he had moved since her last check in the early hours after midnight. "Good," she breathed, still holding on to the doorknob, warring with herself over what to do next.

Leave him to sleep? Wake him to ensure he wasn't comatose? Stand here and stare at the highly unusual and hugely stareworthy sight of a naked man in her bed?

Not *my* bed, she corrected quickly. And not quite naked.

She had, after all, done the undressing. After she'd managed to rouse him with a solid elbow to his ribs. After she'd recovered from the shock of finding herself pressed deep into the thick eiderdown by his relaxed weight.

Heat tingled through her skin as she eyed that same relaxed weight in the yellow-tinged light of early morning. The long stretch of his legs outlined beneath the loosened bedclothes. The bare olive skin of his back, exposed all the way down to the dip below his waist. Broad shoulders and nicely muscled arms spread high and looped around his pillow.

His head was turned away, his face hidden by the dark sweep of his hair. Not sleep mussed like hers—she lifted a hand to the tangled curls—but as long and sleek and smooth as the rest of him. Her hand stilled mid tidying-comb, her gaze riveted on his hand, on the long fingers that loosely gripped one corner of his pillow.

The same fingers she'd felt, last night, flex ever so slightly against her breast.

Awareness tingled warm in her skin, thick in her belly, heavy in her breasts, as she remembered the heat of his body against hers, the heavy slough of his breath, the low moan that had sounded almost sybaritic. Because he was lying down and a matter of seconds away from sleep, not because he'd landed facedown on top of her!

Cat shook her head and huffed a disdainful breath at herself, much the same as she'd done last night right before she elbowed him aside. Then, when he'd looked like falling asleep where he rested, she'd pulled back the bedclothes and made him comfortable.

Starting with the shirt, ending with the jeans, she'd stripped him. Right down to a pair of white cotton boxers. The snug-fitting variety.

Cat's fingers tightened on the doorknob. She closed her eyes a second, warm from the core right out to her skin, with the force of *not* remembering his outline in the semidarkness, the brush of her fingers against hot skin, against hair-rough legs, against the smooth cotton of his underwear.

Crikey.

She started to turn, to leave, then stiffened at the sound of life from the bed. A muffled movement of sheets…or of a body moving against sheets. Her eyes rocketed back to the bed.

Rafe Carlisle was stirring.

His lazy stretch started with a tensing in his shoulders and eased down his backbone, lifting the tight arc of his backside and kicking one leg free of the bedclothes. Cat held her breath in a tense mix of anticipation and apprehension, but he didn't turn his head. He settled in a reverse ripple of muscles, all olive-skinned, languid beauty against her snowy white sheets.

Still asleep, she deduced after another minute, and she suddenly felt uncomfortable standing there watching him. It wasn't as if he knew, but nonetheless she felt as if she was taking advantage. And standing around watching was not at all like her.

Galvanized into action, she hurried back to her room where she dressed, plaited her hair and splashed her face with cold water. In practical clothes and ready to face her working day, Cat felt much more like herself. Her first task was to check for storm damage and assess the state of the roads so she could work out the quickest way to get Rafe Carlisle out of here.

Alone again, with nothing to worry about but her own set of troubles, she would truly feel like herself again.

After the previous night, the thought of getting outside and doing something more active than checking her patient's pulse rate and pupil reaction beckoned as brightly as the spring after-storm sunshine. Cat hit the back veranda at such a pace she almost tripped over the red-and-tan Kelpie waiting on the welcome mat.

The startled dog jumped to attention, tail wagging, instantly alert. A smile curved Cat's mouth as she dropped to her haunches and scratched his neck. This was the only male she was used to seeing first thing in the morning.

"And a mighty handsome male you are, too."

Bach only put up with the petting to humor her, then he gave a let's-go yip and trotted down the steps where he waited, rocking from side to side, eager to start work.

"Okay, I'm coming, I'm coming." She pulled on her boots, still smiling at Bach as she straightened...until she caught sight of the branch that had collapsed across her fence. "Blast."

On closer inspection the branch turned out to be half a tree—a lot more than one strapping woman could shift on her own. It would have to wait. What worried her more than her flattened fence was the merry havoc such a strong wind might have wrought on a light plane.

"That," she told Bach, "is where we're heading first, mate."

Halfway to the airstrip, she heard her call sign over the UHF radio and recognized the laconic voice of her neighbor's foreman. Bob Porter was a good man, despite working for the king of reptilian life forms, Gordon Samuels. A good friend of her father's, Bob made a point of looking out for her, especially since she'd been living on her own and running Corroboree without any permanent help.

They swapped greetings and rainfall measurements before she asked about the state of Samuels's airstrip.

"You expecting a visitor?" Bob asked.

"I have one already." She explained, long-story-short, about the man asleep in her guest room. "I imagine he could have a plane out here to collect him in a matter of hours."

"Well, it ain't landing anywhere around here," Bob drawled. "Not today or tomorrow."

Blast. "I'll have to take him into Bourke then."

"You in a hurry to get rid of this bloke for any reason?"

Yes, he's a distraction. "No, except he's concussed and should see a doctor."

"Hang on a sec."

In less than that second, his wife was on the radio. "I'm going in to town later, Cat. I wouldn't mind a passenger if that helps you out."

"You bet it does." Cat didn't know if she had enough fuel to make the trip herself, and she sure couldn't book anything else up. Not when she hadn't paid her last bill. Not when she didn't know when she would have the money to pay it. "Call me when you're leaving, Jen, and I'll meet you at the cross-roads."

Ninety minutes later Cat shifted the designer overnight bag she'd found in the Cessna from right hand to left, squared her shoulders and knocked on her guest room door. This time she *would* wake him. He'd slept long enough and she needed to know he was all right. She needed him dressed, fed and ready to go when Jennifer Porter called.

Again, no answer.

She edged the door open and found the bedclothes flung back, the bed empty. Her attention flew straight to the bathroom door. She couldn't hear any sound of activity from beyond—no hiss of the shower, no running water, no telltale clank of pipes.

What if he'd done the wonky thing again? What if he'd passed out in there? What if he'd knocked his head falling?

"What if you get your butt over there and find out?" Cat muttered. It was the logical thing to do, the sensible thing to do, the practical thing to do…which all added up to the Cat thing to do.

And she would do it, right after she put his bag down. And neatened the bed. Not that she was procrastinating. Much.

She was smoothing the bottom sheet and pretending not to notice the lingering warmth from his body when she sensed or heard…something. Slowly she straightened and turned and there he was. Standing in the bathroom doorway, watching her. Wearing nothing but the gleam of residual moisture from his shower.

Cat didn't think about looking away. He was, after all, something to behold. And she was, after all, completely beholden. Then he cleared his throat and she realized how long she'd been staring and gave an apologetic caught-out shrug.

"I brought your luggage." She moistened her dry lips and gestured behind her, to where she'd left his bag. "From the plane. I thought you might appreciate some, ah, clothes."

Despite that rather pointed comment, he took his own sweet time reaching for a towel and wrapping it around his hips. He seemed as comfortable in the altogether as she was in her Wranglers. That, she supposed, came with the territory when one possessed the body of a Greek god.

"Thanks." His big smile matched the body. Perfectly. "For bringing my bag."

She probably murmured, "You're welcome," or something equally asinine.

Or she might not have, since she'd become totally involved in watching him rake his hair back from his face as he strolled out of the bathroom. He came right up to the bed, to her side, and her mind went completely blank for a second or three. She forced herself to focus, to think. She couldn't just stand there staring at the dark finger tracks in his shiny wet hair.

Or pretending not to stare.

"You're looking good," she said. Then silently cringed at how that could be taken. Ugh. "In comparison to last night," she added quickly.

He looked as if he knew exactly why she'd felt the need to clarify. The knowledge glinted in his eyes, in the teasing quirk at the corners of his mouth. "What a difference a night makes. I slept like a baby."

No, Cat thought, not a baby. There was something altogether too wicked, too knowing, completely not innocent, about this man for any baby analogy to stick. "For ten hours straight," she said.

"That long? Why didn't you wake me?" Slowly, reflectively, he rubbed his stubbled jaw. "The Sleeping Beauty way would have been nice."

"Excuse me?"

"While I was in the shower I remembered you calling me that in the plane." His gaze drifted to her mouth. "Isn't there supposed to be a kiss involved? Or am I muddling my fairy tales?"

"You were conscious?" *Oh, man, what else did I say? And where did I have my hands at the time?*

Damn his smooth, knowing hide, he grinned at her. "Must have been something about your magic touch."

"I should have left you there!"

"Nah. You enjoyed playing nurse too much."

"Let me think about that...." Cat tapped a finger against her chin. "Did I enjoy your whining? Nope. Prying your eyes open so I could test your pupils? Nope. Getting crushed when you fell on top of me? Nope again."

"I fell on you?"

The man remembered one murmured line while coming out of unconsciousness but he didn't remember lying thigh to thigh, hip to hip, hand to breast with her? Cat shook her head. "I was trying to get you into bed."

"I gather you succeeded?"

"Eventually."

One dark brow arched skeptically—as if he didn't quite believe he'd have put up a fight—and then he gestured toward his clothes, the ones she'd folded and placed on the bedside table. "And you undressed me?"

"Eventually."

He shook his head slowly, almost solemnly. "Sorry I missed that."

Oh, he was good. The deep note of sincerity, the way he looked into her eyes. Cat looked right back and wondered how many women had fallen into those sea-green depths and drowned. Not her. She might live in the arid outback, but she wasn't so parched that she'd swim with sharks.

"I'm not," she said, smiling a little, letting him know she had his measure. "It was…interesting. With you all but unconscious."

He laughed, a rich two-note sound of surprise that ended on a slight wince.

Cat's enjoyment of the moment, the bantering, his laughter, sobered instantly. "How does your head feel?"

"Like it got hit by a plane. Here," he invited. "Feel for yourself."

The instant he ducked his head, the mood dipped, too, slowing and swelling with sensuality. She breathed the scent of his nearness—her soap, her shampoo, but all different on his skin, in his hair. And she was suddenly aware, all over again, that he wore only a towel and that his skin was bare and warm, and that he was waiting for her to touch him.

His head, silly. He only invited you to feel the bump on his head.

Gingerly she palpated the lump, breath held, concern for his injury overriding her preoccupation with the slippery wet strands of his hair, with those damn tracks her own fingers itched to trace. With his sudden stillness and the sense of a new tension in the air.

"Well?" he asked, straightening slowly.

"Does it still ache?"

His eyes narrowed with suspicion. "That depends."

"On?"

"Whether a yes gets me more of your tender loving touch—" Rafe picked up her hand and ran his thumb lightly across her fingertips before releasing it "—or more of that light in my eyes."

"Testing your responses was on doctor's order. If I could have gotten you to hospital, they'd have done the same."

"Except with significantly less wattage."

She opened her mouth, then shut it, as his point about the flashlight's power sunk in. "That's my only torch. And it doesn't appear to have done you any harm. Anyone else would have had a corker of a black eye."

"The cold compress helped."

"I guess." Her gaze softened a little, relenting, relaxing. "What about the rest of you? You're not stiff or sore anywhere else?"

Oh, yeah, she realized how *that* could be taken about a second after the words left her lips. And it wasn't in Rafe's nature to let such a choice opportunity slide. He cocked a brow. "Would you like to check?"

"I'm going to pretend I didn't hear that."

Rafe shrugged. "You can't blame a guy for trying."

She gave him a look that said she could. "It was a god-awful line. You should be ashamed."

"Harsh."

"But honest."

Conceding her point, he tapped two fingers against his temple. "Can we blame it on damage to my head?"

She smiled, but there was a worried edge to the gaze that followed his gesture. A knowledge that while he joked about head damage, it had been a very real concern to her in those long hours of the night.

"I haven't thanked you," he said, watching her turn to pick up his bag. She set it on top of the bed.

"For bringing your bag? I think you did that earlier. I'll leave you to get dressed, then." She started to turn, preparing to leave, but Rafe caught her by the arm and waited for her surprised gaze to swing back to his.

"Not only the bag," he said quietly. "Thank you for rescuing me. Thank you for bringing me into your home and continuing with the observations even after I begged you to give it up. Thank you, Catriona."

She shrugged and shifted uneasily within his grip. "Anyone would have done the same."

"I know a lot of women—" she rolled her eyes in an I-bet-you-do way that Rafe ignored "—and most of them wouldn't have known how to get into that plane, let alone thought to get me out." With his thumb he traced a jagged white scar across the back of her hand. Then he smiled to ease the new note of gravity in the mood. "Most of them would have been afraid they'd break a nail."

"I dare say I'm nothing like most of those women you know."

That went without saying. No fawning, no flirting, not even the hint of a come-on. Most of the women he knew would have taken immediate, unsubtle advantage of his state of undress, but not Catriona McConnell. She was, indeed, a novelty. "When I picked your airstrip, I chose well."

She made a scoffing sound and tugged at her hand until he released her. "Any one of my neighbors would have helped you. And *their* strips wouldn't have wrecked your plane!"

"The landing gear malfunctioned. I was never going to land smoothly."

Eyes wide and appalled, she stared up at him. Her face seemed to have paled a shade, so the smattering of freckles across the bridge of her nose stood out starkly. "Your landing gear malfunctioned? You could have crashed? *Badly?*"

"Hey," Rafe said softly, reaching for her. But she was already backing away, hands held up in classic don't-touch mode. "I didn't mean to frighten you. I was never going to crash-land."

"How do you know that?"

"Because I'm too good a pilot."

She huffed out an incredulous breath. "Well, at least we know your ego wasn't damaged."

"Why do I have the feeling it will suffer if I stick around here much longer?"

From the doorway she paused long enough to cut him a look that perfectly illustrated his point. "Lucky for your ego, you won't be."

Three

"**W**hat is it with you guys and that whole macho 'I'm too good a pilot' business?"

Cat paused in ratting through her pantry for ingredients—anything!—to add to her breakfast hodgepodge and glared at the only male present and therefore answerable. Bach, however, had nothing to say in his gender's defense. He merely tilted his broad canine head and looked curious. Or puzzled. Or possibly both.

"Have you any idea how that cavalier attitude bothers other people?" *How it robs their breath and turns their stomachs sick with dread? Even when they're virtual strangers?*

Halfway across her kitchen, hands filled with cans and condiments, she stopped and frowned, disturbed by the extremity of her reaction to the idea that Rafe Carlisle could have crash-landed.

Must have been the timing, she justified. The surprise element. Plus after seeing him in all his glory he just seemed too vital, too larger than life, to imagine damaged and scarred. Or cold and lifeless.

"Too good a pilot?" With an unladylike snort, she dumped her ingredients on the bench top. "Lucky is more like it!"

Up until that disclosure about his landing-gear malfunction, she'd been handling herself so well, too. Hardly turning a hair when she'd caught him in the buff. Holding her own in the ensuing exchange. Then he'd gone and turned all serious with the thank-you speech, as if she'd done something special.

Well, it was no news flash that Cat McConnell didn't do special. She did capable, she did practical, and some people said she could do stubborn better than anyone. But she sure did not do up-close, skin-tingling, hand-holding seriousness with seminude strangers.

No wonder she'd reacted so intensely to the landing-gear shocker. No wonder the breath had caught in her lungs while her stomach roiled with—

The microwave timer pinged, startling her out of her unsettling memories.

Wake up, Cat, you have breakfast to finish. A guest to get on his way. Normalcy to be returned.

But as she crossed the kitchen to check on the concoction of minced beef and sundries she was nuking, her gaze caught on the photo on the fridge. Drew Samuels with his lopsided grin and black Resistol and laidback cowboy charm.

No, not normalcy. She doubted her life would ever feel normal again. Not if her best friend, her only lover, had let her down as badly as she feared.

"Lucky I've got you," she told Bach, "to keep my faith in males from going completely down the gurgler."

Ears pricked, her dog pattered to her side and growled deep in his chest. Not so much in understanding as in hunger, Cat noted, since she'd lifted the lid on the nuked breakfast dish. Steam spiraled to her nose, piquant, aromatic, and she dipped in a spoon and lifted it, cautiously, to her lips. Tasted. Cocked her head in the dog's direction.

"Not too bad, considering." Considering the amount of scrambling she'd done to find anything substantial enough to feed a man who'd eaten nothing the previous night.

Whimpering, Bach touched a paw to her leg and gave her the big doggy-eyed look.

"Oh, please!" She rolled her eyes and saw him out the door. "I'll get you something in a tick, mate. This is for the guest and I doubt there'll be any leftovers."

Since the guest looked like a man of appetite.

Cat expelled a breath, a swift wisp of air that matched the swing of the door closing behind her dog. She rested her shoulders against the door's solid weight for a moment. Closed her eyes. Rafe Carlisle, she mused, looked like a man with all manner of appetites, food being but one of them.

And it struck her, standing there in the very real surrounds of her kitchen, her home, her niche, how surreal this all was. Everything from Gordon Samuels's revelation about the origin of the money she'd borrowed from Drew, through to watching one of the princes of the outback drop out of the sky, and on to this morning when she'd unwittingly eyed his impressive, um, scepter.

To top it all off, here she was making breakfast for him. Rafe Carlisle. One of Australia's highest-profile playboys, a former Bachelor of the Year, a socialite pin-up who dated actresses and swimsuit models. Oh, how she'd love to share *that* tasty tidbit with her stuck-up stepsisters!

Smiling—ruefully, given she tried to avoid seeing those witches whenever possible—she opened her eyes and pushed off the door.

And jolted to startled attention when she realized that she was no longer alone. The former Bachelor of the Year lazed against the doorjamb on the opposite side of the kitchen, looking so languid and comfortable that she wondered how long he'd been there.

"Ready for breakfast?" she asked, refusing to be rankled. She had, after all, watched him sleep. And he was, after all, now fully dressed.

In a smooth unraveling of long limbs and relaxed muscles—Cat fought to suppress a strong visual of those muscles bare-skinned, as she'd seem them earlier, rippling into lazy motion—he straightened and came into the room. Right past the table, which she'd already set, to rest his hips against the bench. To watch her fill the toaster and turn on the kettle and stir the mystery mince.

He leaned close and drew a long, appreciative sniff.

Then—oh, crikey—he rubbed his belly and made the same sound she remembered from the night before, when he'd fallen into the soft folds of her nanna's handmade quilt.

It was a sound that went with croissants or frittata or eggs benedict served on a sun-drenched terrace. The sound of a man who came to breakfast wearing designer jeans and a butter-colored knit that looked soft enough to melt under the strong outback sun. A sound too luxurious, too rich, too sensuous for her utilitarian kitchen and her tossed-together breakfast.

A sound too rich for Cat, which made it easy to dismiss.

"You cook, too?" he asked.

"Save the praise until after you've tasted," she said matter-of-factly. "I've not been shopping in a while, so this is whatever I could find. It's not gourmet cuisine."

Not that she was apologizing. He was bloody lucky she'd found anything.

When he didn't respond, she glanced sideways and found him looking at her—no, not so much looking as giving her the once-over. Lifting her chin, she met his examination head-on but he didn't look the least chagrined. In fact a smile kicked at the corner of his mouth, not apologetic, just caught out and not caring.

The toast popped, distracting them both, but Cat shot him one last raised-eyebrow glance. "If you're finished with the inspection, take a seat and I'll bring you breakfast."

"And if I'm not...?"

"Take a seat, anyway—" she marched past him and deposited the casserole dish in the center of the table "—you can finish while you eat."

"Are you going to join me?"

"In a tick."

He waited, watched, and only sat after Cat had finished making the tea and taking her own seat opposite. Nice manners, she admitted, a trifle grudgingly since that only indicated two things: he'd been brought up well, and he'd shared a lot of breakfasts with a lot of ladies. Most of whom wouldn't have served him minced beef.

There was a moment when he pushed up his sleeves, and her gaze became riveted on the details. The dark hair on his forearms. The silver links of an expensive-looking watch. His long elegant fingers. The remembered warmth of his touch on her arm and stroking the back of her hand.

Then he caught *her* looking, and the moment stretched with a warm awareness that quickly morphed into awkwardness—on Cat's side of the table, at least—as she poured tea and fussed with the food. A stranger sat at her table, long fingers folded around the handle of one of *her* mugs. *Her* cutlery was transporting the food she had prepared to his mouth, touching his lips, his tongue.

The intimacy of it all shivered through her like quicksilver. More intimate even than before, in the bedroom, although perhaps this disquieting sensation was just the whole twenty-four hours catching up with her.

Whatever the reason, she didn't much like it. Whatever the reason, she had to get over it and start acting more like herself again.

"Relax, Catriona." His mouth quirked, amused and reassuring at the same time. "I know I'm starving, but I promise not to bite."

"Easy for you to say."

His fork paused, halfway to his mouth. "About biting?"

"About relaxing. You aren't the one with a strange man sitting at your breakfast table!"

"I should hope not," he drawled. "Strange women are much more my taste."

"I thought you didn't bite."

He laughed at that, the same rich sound of appreciation as earlier in his bedroom. Cat wasn't sure which affected her more—the warm-honey tone of his laughter or the fact that he appreciated her quick retort. Whichever, the man was lethal.

Lethal and obviously as hungry as he'd intimated, given the way he tucked back into his breakfast. And since the short exchange of banter—plus his rather gratifying appetite—had settled her uneasiness, Cat joined him in several minutes of almost companionable eating. She, too, was starving.

"Glad you've gotten over the strange-man thing."

Cat stopped chewing.

"I wondered about that before," he continued, piling his plate with seconds. "When you were in my bedroom."

"Wondered about…what?" she asked slowly, suspiciously.

"If you lived here alone. And if so, why you weren't more concerned about having a strange man in your house."

"I can look after myself."

"Yeah?"

She met his eyes with unflinching directness. "I've lived here on my own for the last four years. So, yeah, I can look after myself."

"You don't find it lonely here, on your own?"

"Sometimes." Her shrug was a bit tight, a bit not so casual, but her direct gaze turned rueful. "Then my stepmother comes to visit and I get over it real quick."

"You have a wicked stepmother?"

"Good guess."

"Any evil stepsisters?"

"Just the two."

Rafe ate in silence for a minute, digesting all she'd said. "And you run this place single-handedly?"

"What," she said, bristling, "you don't think I'm capable?"

Rafe held up his hands—with knife and fork—in mock defensiveness. "Hey, keep your panties on. That's not what I meant."

"Yeah, well, if I had a dollar…"

"For every man who didn't think you capable?"

"Every*body*," she growled. "No cause to be gender specific."

"Well," Rafe started slowly, carefully picking his way around what was obviously a sore spot. "You've got to admit it's not the usual career choice for a young woman."

"It's all I've ever wanted to do, since I was a little girl."

"You didn't want to be a ballerina or a supermodel?"

"Oh, please!" She didn't exactly roll her eyes, but the gesture was implicit as she rocked back in her chair, a mug of tea cradled in her hands. "Do I look like the supermodel type?"

Trick question, Rafe decided. Wisely he let it slide right by. "You must have had some fantasy occupation, though. I was going to be a fighter pilot."

"See *Top Gun* one too many times?"

"Is that possible?" Smiling, he met her eyes across the remains of their breakfast. "Come on, I've shared my boyhood fantasy. Your turn, Catriona."

"Cat," she corrected. "Everyone calls me Cat."

"I'm not everyone."

This time she did roll her eyes. Then she surprised him by admitting, "I did go through a rodeo stage once."

"You wanted to be a cowgirl?" In jeans and check shirt, with her freckled nose and her hair tightly braided, that wasn't a stretch. All she needed was the big hat and boots.

"A cowgirl? Are you kidding?"

"A rodeo clown?"

Over the rim of her mug she grinned at him, genuine amusement lighting her eyes. "A bull rider, actually."

"I should have known." Rafe shook his head, entertained by the notion but not surprised. His gaze drifted away, toward the kitchen and the picture he'd noticed earlier. "Don't suppose that has anything to do with the cowboy on your fridge?"

"Not really."

"Is he your boyfriend?"

A stillness tightened her expression, and Rafe was surprised to feel an echoing tension in his body as he waited for her answer. As she lifted her mug and took a long deliberate sip before lowering it to answer. "He's a...friend."

Ahh. "A friend you'd like as more?"

She snorted. "A friend I thought *was* more!"

The front legs of her chair hit the floor with a sharp rap, and she was halfway to her feet, gathering cutlery and plates before Rafe stopped her with one hand over both of hers. "I didn't mean to hit a nerve."

Her eyes whipped to his. "You didn't."

Oh, yes, he had. "Where is he now, your cowboy?"

Beneath his hands he felt her tension, felt it gather then ease as if by force of will. She slumped back into her chair, exhaled on a relenting sigh. "Drew's my neighbor—*was* my neighbor. We grew up together. We went out for a while. Then he went to America, on the rodeo circuit."

Her flat, just-the-facts delivery didn't fool Rafe. The neighbor, the ex, the cowboy with the big black hat had let her down. Badly.

"You want me to find this Drew, beat him up for you?" he asked, wanting to make her smile again, and rather liking the notion of playing her champion. "I do owe you."

"For coming to your rescue?" She smiled, not the dazzler of before but a smile that held a sharp wry edge. She tugged her hands free and rocked back in her chair. "You want to hear something funny? Yesterday, when I heard your plane, I thought you were Drew."

"You were expecting him?"

She shrugged. "Not so much expecting as hoping."

"Ah, so finding me must have been a huge disappointment."

"It wasn't all bad," she said with that same wry smile. "At least you and your head gave me something else to worry about. I didn't have much time to be disappointed."

"Ouch," he murmured, without a lot of conviction. "I knew you wouldn't be good for my ego."

"I imagine your ego is in as fine shape as the rest of you." And with that matter-of-fact diagnosis, she started packing up their plates and taking them to the kitchen.

Rafe bit his tongue. He didn't need to ask how she knew about his fine shape. She'd seen pretty much all of it in the bathroom earlier. But he did need to ask what she'd meant earlier, before she walked out of his bedroom.

"The last time we were discussing my ego, you said I wouldn't be sticking around long."

"That's right. A neighbor's going in to Bourke today. I've arranged a lift for you."

It was Rafe's turn to rock back in his chair. She sure hadn't wasted any time. "When?"

She looked up from the sink where she was stacking dishes and smiled. "Not too long. I imagine by the time you've finished clearing up the table and washing these, Jen will have called with an exact time."

With thirty years of practice, Rafe had perfected his helpless-male routine. Catriona McConnell wasn't the first woman to see right through it, but she'd done so with a remarkable indifference to his charm. Twenty minutes later Rafe still wore a rueful grin. She really was something else!

When he'd stared cluelessly at the sink and murmured, "Washing dishes, huh? This should be interesting," she didn't roll her eyes and nudge him aside so she could take over—which is what he'd been angling for.

He'd tried another tack. "I've never done this before. I don't suppose you'd care to give some hands-on instruction?"

"Oh, I'm pretty sure you're smart enough to work it out for yourself."

"What if I break stuff?"

"My stuff is hardly Limoges," she'd flung over her shoulder on her way to the door. "But if it makes you feel any better, I'll add any breakages to your bill."

"That should make me feel better? With this head?"

Hand on door, she'd paused, frowning. "Your head's aching? Perhaps you should go and lie down."

"Will you bring me a cold compress and take my pulse, Nurse?"

She made an impatient sound, tongue against teeth. "Don't you ever give up?"

"What?"

"The lines. We both know they're wasted on me."

Rafe shook his head sadly. "You're a hard woman, Catriona McConnell."

She'd smiled and thanked him, as if that were the greatest of compliments, before closing the door behind her. Ten seconds later it opened again—and, yeah, she caught him still grinning and shaking his head over that exchange—so she could remind him about the phone calls he'd been deliberately forgetting.

"The phone is in my office—" she pointed off to her right "—through that second doorway over there."

"Will the calls be on my bill?"

"Of course. Knock yourself out."

Rafe had winced at her unfortunate wording, but that was all for show.

After finishing his phone calls, as he headed out the door where she'd disappeared earlier, he remembered her words with a grin of approval. It didn't surprise him that he liked her—he rarely met a woman he didn't like on some level— but it surprised him how much this smart-as-a-cardshark woman tickled his fancy.

On the back porch he paused to look around, seeing her place for the first time. Seeing what lay beneath and beyond the debris scattered by last night's storm with another jab of surprise. The paint peeling from the outside walls. The empty garden beds. Beyond the back fence, what looked to be the remains of an orchard, the trees long dead. Catriona's home wore an air of disrepair like a patched-up coat and he hadn't expected that. She seemed so on top of everything.

Then he remembered the moment at the breakfast table, when he'd asked about her cowboy and he'd felt the tension—and her disillusionment—hovering in the kitchen air. Things weren't any more shipshape in her world than in his, and it struck him that fate—or his most faithful mistress, Lady Luck—might have landed him here for a reason. Nine times out of ten he would have backed himself to outrace a storm. But yesterday he'd been flying with his mother's words soft in his memory.

Take care, Rafe. Please, don't do anything harebrained that you might come to regret!

He knew she'd been talking about more than his daredevil ways with a joystick, yet her message of caution and the accompanying concern—in eyes already pierced with grief from her husband's recent death—had led him to search out a strip when the storm billowed quicker and wilder than predicted.

That strip was Catriona McConnell's.

And as he crossed the yard with its random patches of would-be lawn, as he sidestepped sheets of roofing steel blown clean off a nearby shed, he decided that fate had put him here for more than washing her dishes. More, even, than shifting the uprooted tree that lay crushing her fence.

This trip had a purpose, one he'd resisted for the first month or more since his father's death. Since he and his two brothers learned about the will's clause and the baby they needed to produce. Needed, not wanted. Rafe couldn't see himself in the role of father, which meant he needed to choose very wisely.

More wisely than Nikki Bates. More wisely than any of the women in his past.

Yup, he decided as his narrowed gaze fixed on Catriona down by the kennels. Fate had come to his rescue in the nick of time.

Four

Cat was sitting cross-legged on the concrete stoop outside her kennel enclosure, her lap filled with sleeping puppies, when she heard the distant slap of the kitchen door closing. Blast. She'd hoped that the washing-up and his phone calls would have kept him occupied for longer. Another five minutes enjoying the simple, comforting warmth of the morning sun and her canine company was all she wanted. Five minutes before she faced up to the consequences and cost of last night's storm. Before making the tough decisions on what to do next, how to find Drew, who to believe.

With a heavy sigh, she lifted one chubby tan body close to her face. "Not that I have any idea where to start on that one, little mate." Everything about her dealings with Drew had turned out to be so much less than she'd bargained for.

For some reason that turned her thoughts right back to Rafe Carlisle, who had turned out to be so much more than she'd bargained for. It was one thing to enjoy looking at him, appreciating his beauty the same as she would a sleek Thoroughbred or an exquisitely formed sculpture or some out-of-her-reach trinket in a shop window. It was another entirely to enjoy his company, to sit at the breakfast table trading quips and confidences. To stick her head through the door and see him with sleeves pushed up, hands in her sink, that lethal grin lifting the corners of his exquisitely formed mouth.

Knowing that *she'd* put the grin there.

That memory mingled with the crunch of his footsteps on the gravel approach, and Cat shivered—not in her skin but somewhere deeper. For a wisp of time she buried her nose in the puppy's fur, absorbing its comforting warmth, centering herself so that when she turned and peered up at him none of that unease showed in her expression…despite the way her heart revved up a gear.

From her position down on the ground, it was a perilously long way up to his face. A long traverse past thighs and hips encased in expensively aged denim. Past that buttercream knit that should have made him look soft but—damn it—didn't. And by the time she'd taken that all in, by the time she'd arrived up at his face with all its dark planes and masculine angles, he was ducking down to her level and reaching out to stroke the puppy in her hands.

"So…Cat is a dog person," he said, sea-green eyes awash with amusement.

Cat tried to smile back, but she was transfixed by those eyes and then by the gentle stroke of one large fingertip over the tiny puppy's head. Snared by the magnetic power of his proximity. Even in the bedroom he hadn't been this close, his head almost grazing hers as he bent to study the bundle of puppies in her lap.

"How many have you got there?" he asked, his voice as slow and mesmerizing as that caress.

"Seven, all up."

"Huh. My lucky number."

Probably another line, but she had to admire the finesse of his delivery. The smooth way he had of drawing her in with what appeared to be genuine attentiveness. Why not enjoy it? Any kind of attentiveness was a novelty, and dogs she could talk about until the cows came home!

"Where's their mama?" he asked, and Cat looked around for Sheba.

"She won't be too far away. Especially if she gets a whiff of a stranger lurking near her babies."

"Ah, a warning. Should I step back slowly, hands in the air? Before or after she bares her teeth?"

Cat smiled. "I think the worst you'll suffer is a severe growling."

"From a mother, growling can be scary stuff."

Although he grinned back at her, she sensed a truth in his words. And glimpsed another element she hadn't bargained for—the disquieting element of Rafe Carlisle in family mode. Carefully she settled the puppy from her hand back with its siblings. "Yeah, well, Sheba's growl is much worse than her bite. She's only ever taken a violent dislike to one man."

"Your cowboy?"

"His father, actually." Cat met his eyes and saw a stillness, a seriousness, she hadn't expected. Saw questions she didn't want to answer…and was saved by the distraction of a low canine whimper. The perfect segue. "Speaking of fathers—" she nodded toward his right "—that's the pups' daddy over there."

As expected, Rafe turned to inspect the daddy. Head on paws, Bach treated them to his best put-upon look and another pitiful whine.

"Oh, please!" Cat shook her head at her dog before explaining to Rafe. "I have to lock him up while Sheba goes for a run, otherwise she won't leave her puppies. Bach thinks it's the height of indignity."

"You called your dog Bark?" he asked on a note of disbelief, although a smile lifted the corners of his lips.

"*B-A-C-H.* Like the composer."

"Awful pun."

"Yes, but *Wag*ner would have been worse."

He laughed at that, a rich rumble of amusement that warmed her from her inside out. Oh, yeah, the man knew how to laugh, how to smile, how to charm. "At least my cat has a dignified name."

That laconic admission whipped her attention from his lips to his eyes. "You have a *cat?*"

His eyes narrowed. "Don't tell me you're one of those dog people who look down their noses at cat owners?"

"Not at all. I just didn't picture you with a cat, is all."

Cat didn't want to picture him with a pet any more than being growled at by his mother. She much preferred her pre-conception of Rafe Carlisle as a superficial, self-obsessed rich kid. Entertaining, likable, highly watchable, but essentially lightweight. She really wished she didn't have to ask, "What is your cat's dignified name?"

"Tolstoy."

"Is he a Russian blue?"

"I have no idea."

"Then why did you name him Tolstoy?" she asked, hope stacked upon hope that he didn't enjoy the classics, because that would be too much on top of all his charm and wit and the pet-ownership thing.

"I didn't. He belonged to a woman I knew. I guess she named him."

Cat's heart put in a funny little kick beat as she wondered what, exactly, the word *knew* meant in Rafe-Carlisle-speak. "And she gave her cat to you?"

"She left, and the next day Tolstoy was back." He gave a careless little shrug, like the shift of spare muscle inside his silk sweater. "Apparently he preferred living with me."

"Didn't she?" Cat asked without thinking.

And when his eyes lifted to hers, when their sea-green

depths glowed with a wicked lick of heat, she wished she *had* thought. Wished she'd bitten her tongue and her curiosity.

"Oh, she liked it well enough," he drawled, and Cat believed she knew why. He would be lethal in bed. As lazy and graceful as that shrug; as knowing and sinful as those eyes.

As hot as the wash of curiosity that streamed through Cat's veins.

She struggled to contain both the heat and the curiosity. Struggled against the crazy itch to reach out and touch the silky strands of his hair, the extravagant fullness of his bottom lip, the stubbly regrowth of dark beard along the sharp line of his jaw.

Methodically, one by one, she folded the fingers that itched to touch into her palm, forming a loose fist, which she rubbed along her thigh. And she reminded herself what this exchange really meant about this man and his life and his lifestyle. *Not for you, Catriona McConnell, not even in your wildest midnight imaginings.*

"So you kept her cat," she said.

"His choice."

Cat was saved from remarking on Tolstoy's taste when Sheba trotted back from her short spell of exercise and took immediate exception to Rafe's presence. "It's okay, baby," she soothed while she quietly transferred the puppies to their kennel. "This is Rafe Carlisle and he's not as big and scary as he looks. He has a cat."

Rafe gave a half grunt of laughter. It didn't surprise her that he felt no need to defend himself against the cat-ownership charge. As she'd already noted, his male ego was in excellent shape.

For an oddly comfortable moment they watched the pups jostle for prime positions at their mother's belly. Odd because she'd thought this might have been awkward in its intimacy…and perhaps it could have been if he'd let the moment, silent but for the muffled sound of suckling, stretch.

Instead he smiled and said, "Hungry little beggars."

"Lucky they've got a good mamma."

But when she finished securing the gate on Sheba's pen and turned, ready to get on with her chores, she found him watching her with unexpectedly serious eyes. It jolted her for a second, that expression, the stillness in his big body, the skip of her heart.

But she kept on moving, picking up the hose and turning on the tap, keen to push whatever that moment was about out of her consciousness. "Did you make your phone calls?" she asked.

"Unfortunately."

His dry tone brought her gaze swinging back to his as she filled the water containers. "Alex wasn't happy then?"

"Why do you suppose I rang my brother?" he asked slowly.

Cat shrugged. "You mentioned him enough times yesterday. I gathered he owns the plane in my paddock…although you kept calling it a jet."

"I did?" Uncertainty clouded his expression, bringing his dark brows together in a confused frown.

"After I got you out of the plane," she explained, "when we were driving back here, you kept repeating yourself. You'd tell me something, then forget and tell me again."

"Did I embarrass myself?"

Oh, the temptation to tease him! It hovered in front of her, a great big shining orb of enticement, too bright to resist. "I crashed the jet." She slurred the words, imitating his voice from the previous day. "Alecsh will be pished."

Rafe winced, and she felt a tiny pang of remorse for teasing him over something so serious. But only a tiny one.

"I gather it is your brother's plane?"

"No. I hired it in Bourke. Alex's jet is safe and sound at the airport. I rang and checked." Expression rueful, he rubbed a hand along his jaw. "If I had crashed the Citation, Alex definitely would have been pissed."

"If you'd crashed a jet, you really wouldn't have to worry about your brother!"

A sobering thought, and one Cat didn't want to revisit. She had no business feeling fright or relief or anything on his behalf. No business feeling *anything* for the man. He flew a private jet, for heaven's sake. He hired a light plane the way other mere mortals hired a car or hailed a cab. At the moment Cat would give her eyeteeth for enough cold hard cash to hire a bicycle!

"You hired the Cessna?" she began as she turned off the tap and coiled the hose. She didn't need to know more about him, but she needed to talk, to consolidate who he was, to chase away the whispery traces of uneasiness that coiled through her gut. Straightening, she found him lounging against the mesh gate of Sheba's pen looking askance. "After you flew Alex's jet to Bourke?"

"That's right. I'd been visiting with my mother."

"She lives on a station, right? In the Northern Territory? I remember reading that somewhere."

"Kameruka Downs," he told her. "We grew up there, my brothers and me. Tomas still lives there and runs the cattle business."

"I read an article about him in *The Cattleman*."

"That's the one," Rafe said slowly as their gazes linked. "I guess you've read a bit about my family here and there."

"A bit."

The classic understatement, Rafe knew, especially when there'd been so much to read in the past couple of months. And when her hazel eyes clouded, when their expression softened with sympathy, he knew she'd been reading that press.

"You lost your father recently," she said. "I'm sorry."

Rafe inclined his head in the briefest acknowledgment. Charles Carlisle might not have been his birth father, but he was the only father he'd known.

"How is your mother coping?"

"Barely." Little point in sugarcoating the truth, not when the gossip media had made a meal of Maura's "increasingly hermitlike existence" in the month after her husband's death. As if her choice to live out of the public eye and her decision not to attend his very public and photographed memorial service painted her eccentric. "Although she might have coped better without Dad's interference."

"Interference?"

Rafe hadn't meant to bring this up yet, but since she'd introduced the topic…since she was studying him with such a cute look of befuddlement…why not answer her question? Why not see where it took him? "He had this notion that a grandchild would abbreviate the grieving process."

Her cute puzzlement turned to a deep frown. "I don't understand."

Rafe could appreciate her confusion. Theirs—his and his brothers'—had been considerable. And heated. Their mother's more so when she found out six weeks later. "When he got sick he added a clause to his will. We didn't know anything about it until afterward."

"When the will was read?"

He nodded. "So, we have twelve months to produce a grandchild for Mau."

"Or you lose your inheritance?"

"Yup."

Her face was a picture of astonishment as she digested this information, as she sifted through the pieces and put it all together as a whole. "You and your brothers," she asked slowly, "do you *all* have to have a baby?"

"The clause specifies only one grandchild among us, but given the short time span and the fact we're all starting from scratch, as it were…we're playing the odds."

They'd made a pact, one in, all in, the same way it had always been between them. No other way seemed fair. No other way gave them the best odds of succeeding.

"So." She cleared her throat. "How's that going?"

Rafe laughed dryly. Trust Catriona to cut straight to the chase. "Tomas has a willing lady but he's being a stubborn fool over it. Alex and Susannah—" he shook his head "—are still trying to find a spare hour in their schedules to get married first."

She raised her brows.

"He's a traditionalist."

"And you? Have you any, um, projects in the making?"

"Why? Are you offering to help me out?"

She laughed and shook her head. "Funny."

"Is that what you think?"

Their gazes locked, and the mocking laughter in her eyes darkened, deepened. "Yes, actually. I do think that's pretty funny."

"Which part?"

"The part where *you* can't find a woman to have your baby. I rather thought they'd be queuing up at your bedroom door!"

"Maybe I'm particular."

She snorted. "What about your cat lady?"

"A possibility…although her husband might object."

"Can't you pay someone?"

"There's a thought," he said slowly, consideringly, even though her throwaway line had dripped with sarcasm. "How much would it take, Catriona?"

She stared back at him, her eyes wide and starting to spark with indignation. "I was kidding, you know! Paying a woman to have your baby so you can inherit more money—that's appalling. It's just plain…wrong. What would the child—" She stopped cold. Gave a short, strangled laugh. "You weren't serious, were you?"

"Do you think my mother would want a grandchild from that kind of a union?" he asked.

She wouldn't. But his mother *would* want a woman who considered the idea appalling and just plain wrong. A woman who'd stand up with her eyes sparking and tell him so. A woman who managed everything from a concussed stranger to driving through a savage storm to copping an eyeful of naked man without missing a beat.

A woman who held a tiny puppy cradled in her hand and who crooned soft words to the agitated mother.

And Rafe?

He liked that this same woman seemed unimpressed by who he was or how much he was worth. He liked the idea that she had never wanted to do anything but live in the outback and run her property. An independent woman who would let him do his own thing....

Slowly he closed the space between them. "We're not doing this to inherit more money, Catriona. We want to keep the Carlisle companies in the family, true, but mostly we want to honor our father's last wish by doing what we can to make our mother happy."

"You said before she'd be happier without his interference."

"I said she might have coped better." He stopped in front of her, not close enough to crowd but close enough to see the responsive skip of pulse in her throat. "Instead she's worried sick about us doing something harebrained."

"Harebrained?"

Rafe smiled. "Her word."

"Like having a baby with an unsuitable woman?"

"Precisely." He cocked his head and pretended to inspect her intently. Eyes narrowed and wary, she looked right back. "Now you, Catriona, would be quite suitable."

"Oh, yeah, sure. And will that be just the one baby with you, or one with each of your brothers, too?"

"You don't want to have kids?"

"Eventually." She shrugged but the effort looked tense, far from casual. "But not today, thanks for asking."

"Pity" was all Rafe said, but he smiled at her answer, at her crisp no-nonsense delivery, at the fact that she'd just made up his mind without knowing it. Convincing her would be a challenge, but he loved nothing better than a worthy adversary.

When she tried to step sideways, he moved with her. First left, then right. She exhaled an exasperated breath, stood her ground, and when her eyes met his, they flashed green with annoyance. "What now?" she asked.

"That tree in your yard…"

It only took a second for her to catch up with his abrupt change in topic. "I assume you mean the one that's not supposed to be in my yard?"

"That's the one. If you point me in the direction of your chainsaw I'll take care of it."

She started shaking her head round about "chainsaw" and was speaking over the top before he finished. "You think I'll let you loose with a dangerous power tool?"

"You let me loose with a dangerous dish mop."

"Funny."

"Come on, Catriona, you can't shift that monster on your own. Your friend will be here soon to take me away. Why not put me to work while you can? Come on," he cajoled, leaning closer, smiling into her eyes. Letting his voice drop a half, silky note. "You know you want to…."

Cat refused to think about what she wanted to do with Rafe Carlisle and his wickedly unsettling suggestions. Since he insisted, she did put him to work, although not with the chainsaw and not without another confrontation. "You were concussed. You should be taking it easy, not doing physical work, let alone with a chainsaw screaming in your ears."

"Don't you have any of those Princess Leia ear muffs for protection?"

Yes, but… "You can't work in those clothes. You'll snag your pretty sweater."

He obliged by taking it off. "Better?"

How much longer did she have to put up with him driving

her crazy? Less than an hour, she told herself as he stood there before her, all fake innocence and bare-chested beauty.

"What if you scratch yourself on the branches?"

"I'm counting on it." He grinned wolfishly. "So you can play nurse again."

Exasperated, she stomped inside and fetched him an old work shirt and insisted he put it on. He did, except the buttons wouldn't do up, and then he ripped both underarm seams hauling away one of the branches she'd lopped.

"Add it to my bill," he said after he tore out the sleeves to give himself more room.

He fashioned one into a bandanna, which, combined with the too-small shirt and the ear-muffs, should have looked silly. Not on Rafe. He looked as if he'd walked right out of a diet cola ad. Cat sighed and went back to work with the chain-saw. At least the tree would soon be gone...and so would he. Gone with his smooth-skinned beauty and his nefarious grins and his way of making her laugh and talk and remember what it was to enjoy company.

Making her forget for hours at a time that she had little to smile about.

A pleasant diversion, she told herself. Extremely pleasant to look at and to talk to...up until he started on the baby thing. That whole exchange had left her feeling weird, unsettled, as if she'd stepped off a roller coaster and hadn't regained her balance. She sneaked a look at him over the decimated remains of the gum tree and felt the same swamping wave churn through her body.

This had nothing to do with muscles that flexed and curved and gleamed with the makings of sweat. This was about the love in his eyes when he talked about his mother, the way he wanted to satisfy his father's last wish, the obvious bond with his brothers. This was about the dreams for her future that had slipped away with Drew—dreams of the babies she would have to make her own family. This was about all she didn't have and all she'd thought she'd got past missing and wanting.

Blast.

She turned off the saw and sat back on her haunches to take a breath. To gather herself because she realized she was shaking. Not tremors on the outside, but that same shivery feeling deep inside she'd felt earlier, only more so. Not good with a chainsaw in one's hands! She pulled her ear protection down around her neck and swiped the back of one hand across her sweaty forehead.

Then she sat up straight, eyes fixed on the vehicle thundering up her drive. Behind her she sensed Rafe's stillness, as if he, too, had stopped work to watch the four-wheel-drive as it bounced across the last cattle grid and disappeared behind the house.

"That must be Jen," she said, even though the Porters drove a crew-cab and Jen hadn't called to say she was on her way. Even though she and her sinking stomach both knew who drove that exact model of Landcruiser. It reappeared, swinging around the back of the house, and she and her sinking stomach both recognized the big bullheaded shape in the driver's seat.

And so did Bach. He appeared out of nowhere in a rush of snarling outrage, intent on chasing the vehicle to a standstill. Carefully Cat stood, chainsaw in her hands. The idea of greeting her visitor, thus armed, held huge appeal.

"Is his name really Jen?" Rafe asked at her side.

"No, his name is Gordon Samuels. He's Jen's boss and my neighbor."

"The cowboy's father," Rafe muttered, obviously clued in by the sight of Bach, teeth bared, three inches from the driver's door. Which explained why that door hadn't yet opened. "I gather you weren't expecting him."

"No," she said with a tight smile. "But if I were a betting woman, I'd lay my last dollar on why he's graced us with his company."

"Us?"

Cat's laugh was short and caustic and had nothing to do with mirth. "You're right. This isn't about us. This is about *you*."

"I've never met the man."

"I dare say he found out you were here from Bob Porter. And now he's here to drive you into Bourke because, well, you are a Carlisle."

Side by side they watched Samuels's motionless silhouette inside the truck for another crawling minute. "Are you going to call your dog off?" Rafe asked.

"I haven't decided."

"I guess it's a pickle of a choice for you."

"How's that?"

"You let your neighbor out and get rid of me. Or you leave him to fester in his own juices and you get to keep me." Eyes glittering with a dangerous light swung slowly to meet hers. "What's it going to be, Catriona? Do I go or do I get to stay?"

Five

Catriona met his gaze with steady directness while she appeared to give that choice due consideration. "Tempting," she murmured, "But…"

Rafe sighed. "There's always a *but,* isn't there?"

"Sadly…yes."

She called her dog off; and after a couple of minutes in her neighbor's company, Rafe wished she hadn't. He'd met a thousand patronizing, self-important, butt-kissing Gordon Samuelses in his time and that was about a thousand too many.

Only too happy to help out a neighbor in need. Would have been here earlier if I'd known Catriona was going to put you to work. Good grief, girl, don't you know who the Carlisles are? Etc, etc, etc.

Apparently, getting one's hands dirty and riding with the hired help was beneath a Carlisle's station in life. Who knew? Still, Rafe accepted his offer of a lift into Bourke in Jennifer Porter's stead, but only so he could put the man's toadying to good use. He had questions to ask; he expected to find Samuels bursting with ready answers.

After a quick shower—he'd have preferred leisurely, but he'd left Catriona and her chainsaw alone with Samuels—there wasn't anything left to do but say goodbye.

Oh, and kiss her.

Distracted by whatever had gone down between her and Samuels while he showered—whatever had made her eyes churn in a dark and angry storm—she didn't see the kiss coming until his head was bending down to hers. By then his hand cupped the back of her head and his fingers were dipping into the thick sections of her braid, and she couldn't escape.

His lips found hers just as her mouth opened to object. Perfect timing, he decided, smiling against her lips. Tasting her tiny gasp of surprise while he stroked his thumb over her sun-warmed hair. It was a short kiss, a sweet kiss, with no body contact but a whole world of connection when their eyes met and held. Rafe felt a jolt of pleasure, not savage, not fierce, not even unexpected.

He knew he'd enjoy kissing his angel of mercy. Knew she'd taste as warm and earthy as she looked and that her eyes would shimmer with a thousand pleasurable possibilities. He wanted to tell her to think about every one—to think about him—when she was alone in her bed, but Samuels cleared his throat and reminded him they weren't alone right now. Which started Bach growling like a turboprop before takeoff.

Catriona made an impatient sound in her throat. "I know, I know," she told her dog. "But he's about to leave, I promise."

Rafe knew she was talking about Samuels and grinned at the edgy snarl to her voice. He fished a card from his pocket and jotted down his contact details. "I'll call you when I get back to Sydney, but these are my numbers, home and office, in case—"

"There's no need."

"Oh, but there is." He folded her fingers around the card she seemed reluctant to take and focused on the solid practicalities instead of the ethereal promise of that kiss. "There's the small matter of the plane I landed in your paddock and then there's the not-so-small matter of my bill."

"I was joking."

"And I'm not. Whether you want or not, I'm going to repay your hospitality, Catriona. You might want to start thinking about how and when."

Restitution was only the first of Rafe's goals for Catriona. During the next sixty minutes, he intended to learn all he could about her—anything to stack the odds in his favor for when he got to the main one. As expected, Gordon Samuels fell all over himself to help.

He learned that she'd inherited the debt-ridden Corroboree from her father while she was still at school. Samuels had managed the station and her stepmother the trust account while she completed her education. Significant, Rafe thought, that she now seemed to hold both parties in extreme contempt.

Samuels told him that since Catriona took over management, she'd struggled to keep her head above water. "I threw her a life buoy but once she sets her mind on something, the girl's as tough to shift as a barnacle."

Catriona might well be stubborn, but she didn't strike him as a fool. Obviously, she needed help badly, so why had she refused to grab ahold of that buoy? There was something going on between her and the Samuelses, more that he needed to discover—more that he would discover—in order to find out what kind of rescue raft she would climb aboard.

Unfortunately, he didn't have much time to launch that raft. Two months and the clock was ticking.

He cut a sideways glance at Gordon Samuels, at the man's tough profile shaded beneath a big western hat, and he remembered the picture on Catriona's fridge. And his certainty that the cowboy had let her down, badly.

The same conviction snared him now. The knowledge that the key to Catriona rested with Drew Samuels.

"So, Gordon," he commenced casually. "Catriona tells me you have a son in America. A bullrider...?"

Cat heard her phone ringing as she stepped out of the shower, and the certainty of who was calling buzzed through her at roughly the same frequency as that strident bell. She wished she could ignore it. Or at least take the time to dry herself instead of bolting, towel in hand, for her office.

Unfortunately, she couldn't. Nor could she stop the trimble in her hand as she picked up the receiver, although she put a choke hold on her unruly anticipation and took a deep breath before attempting to speak.

All this just because the man had dropped in a cursory thank-you-and-goodbye kiss!

"Hello," she said, sounding quite calm, considering.

"You really should get a message bank, Catriona." No hello, no other preliminary—not that Rafe needed to identify himself. Who else drew her name out over all four syllables in that thoroughly extravagant way?

"You've been trying to call?"

"I told you I would." She heard the smile in his voice, pictured those full lips quirked at the corners. Remembered their pressure against hers with a flutter of heat somewhere deep inside. "You must have started early this morning."

"Sixish," she confirmed.

"Guess I just missed you then."

"You called at *sixish?* I meant in the morning!"

He laughed, a soft, low sound that vibrated through her like a cat's purring. "I was down at Randwick Racecourse before sunrise, watching Alex's next champion gallop. I called on my way home at sixish. Then again at sevenish. Again over lunch."

Whoa.

"I thought I might catch you in. Don't you ever eat?"

Only when I have food in the house. "Only on odd-numbered days."

"So, you haven't eaten tonight?"

"If I say no, will you buy me dinner?" A safe question, with him five hundred miles away in Sydney. Safe and easy to swap banter with him at the other end of a phone call.

"How long would it take you to get ready?" he asked.

"For a free meal, I'd go as I am."

"And how's that, Catriona?" His deep voice lingered over her name in a way that made her very aware of her nakedness. And of how she'd been daydreaming under the shower about seeing him right out of the shower.

Daydreaming about him using that princely body to pay her back for her hospitality.

An acceptable fantasy, she'd justified sometime during the night when it first slid steamy and alluring into her imagination, since it was only a fantasy. Acceptable, too, because it stopped her thinking about that disturbing conversation out at the kennels. Stopped her daydreaming about things like, oh, having the man's baby.

"What *are* you wearing?" he prompted.

Cat snorted and propped the receiver between ear and shoulder so she could wrap herself in the towel. "Don't tell me you get your jollies from women describing their underwear."

"Usually—" he paused and the sound of movement made her think he was settling back, getting comfortable "—I get my jollies taking off women's underwear."

That predictable response rolled smooth and silky from his tongue—the same way she imagined him rolling underwear from her body. Except he hadn't meant *her* underwear, and the notion of his expert hands on other women's underwear—on other women's bodies—turned her next provocative response to bitter-tasting ashes.

She sat heavily in her desk chair and gripped the front of her towel more firmly. Fun time was over. "Why were you calling all day, anyway?" she asked. "Is there a problem with salvaging the plane?"

"No. They're sending someone out tomorrow…but that's not why I called. I need to settle my bill."

He'd called half a dozen times about that? "You do understand I was joking."

"You do understand I was serious about repaying your hospitality."

"There's no need," she said quickly. Her heart was starting to beat with similar speed. She was getting bad vibes about this. "I don't need any payment."

There was the briefest pause before he asked, "Are you sure about that, Catriona?"

Grimacing, she pinched the bridge of her nose between finger and thumb. *Gordon Samuels and his big mouth. That's where the bad vibes stemmed from!* "You shouldn't believe everything you hear."

"And what is it you think I've heard?"

"It's a long drive into Bourke," she said dryly, "so I expect you heard a lot."

"Samuels told me you were doing it tough. Should I believe that?"

He'd been there. He'd stepped over roofing iron blown from her rundown buildings. Did he really have to ask? "Did my good neighbor tell you why I'm broke?"

"He mentioned drought years after your father's death—"

"That's not what I meant, unless you count the way his drought mismanagement drove Corroboree into the ground!" She inhaled sharply in a last-ditch effort to contain the bitterness that had crept into her tone. "Actually, I meant more recently. Like in the last month."

Silence. She'd thought as much. And although every instinct hammered at her to shut the hell up, she couldn't. Who knew what crap Samuels had spun during that drive? It shouldn't have mattered what Rafe Carlisle had heard and whether that had influenced his opinion of her, but it did. She'd lost so much over the last several years. Pride was one of the few things she had left.

"I took money from his son. A personal loan, I suppose, although—" She stopped cold, realizing suddenly that she didn't want to share the "although" because that included the part about giving Drew her body and her love and her trust. The part where they'd lain in her bed and talked about running Corroboree together. When he offered her the money, she took it as his commitment to their future, although her pride had insisted she call it a loan.

"Although?" he prompted.

"Last month Samuels told me the money was his. He says he wants it repaid, but what he really wants is Corroboree."

"Is the money his?"

"I don't know." Cat sighed and pinched the bridge of her nose again. Harder. "I've been trying to contact Drew to find out what's going on, but he's not answering my messages. He could be anywhere, competing or on the road. He mightn't have e-mail access, he might have changed his mobile phone number, he mightn't be getting my messages."

Rafe said nothing for a long time, and that pause seemed to resonate with the desperate ring of her words.

Cat squeezed her eyes shut and grimaced. "I'm sorry. I didn't mean to tell you all that. I just wanted to set the record straight, given what Samuels might have told you. I just opened my mouth and out it all came."

"Don't apologize, Catriona. I like that you've taken me into your confidence."

Is that what she'd done? Taken this man—this stranger from another world—into her confidence? Like a friend? She coiled the phone cord around her hand while tendrils of unease coiled around her stomach.

"So, what are you doing to set this straight?"

"What can I do?" She huffed out a ragged little laugh. "Look, Rafe, you don't have to concern—"

"Does Samuels have proof that he loaned you anything?"

Apparently he *did* have to concern himself, and Cat hovered for a second, twisting and untwisting the phone cord, unsure about this confidence thing. Perhaps talking it over with a stranger, an outsider, was a good thing. Perhaps he'd shake loose an angle she'd missed.

"Did you sign anything?"

"No," she admitted, sinking deeper into the chair and closing her eyes. "I took the money from Drew on a handshake agreement, but Samuels says he signed the loan over to him. How could that work?"

"Sounds like you need legal advice."

A fine idea if she had the money to pay for such advice! "What I need is to talk to Drew."

"Have you thought about hiring someone to find him? Or going over there to track him down?"

She laughed without mirth. "If I had a dollar for every time I've thought about getting over there and grabbing him by the shirtfront and shaking the damn truth out of him, I'd be able to afford the airfare."

"What if you had the airfare?" he asked after a tick of pause, and Cat sucked in a breath and straightened her back in bristling denial.

"Oh, no, Rafe. You are not going to pay for a ticket."

"Are you too stubborn to accept help?"

"I can't accept *your* help."

"Yet I had to accept yours."

"That was different," she fired back. "If I ever knock myself out landing a plane, I will accept your help in a heartbeat."

"Do you remember taking me to bed?" he asked softly. Cat swallowed. *In her fantasies, yes.* "You told me you weren't a difficult person."

Oh, *that* taking him to bed. Taking his weight when his balance gave out. Stumbling at the door to her bedroom. Shaking her head when he refused to allow one last check of his responses.

And he'd asked if *she* was always this difficult!

"Let me help you with this, Catriona." His voice changed, as if he'd shifted position again, as if he held the receiver closer to his mouth. As if he were right here, mouth close to her ear, enticing her to let him do all kinds of things for her. To her. With her. Cat shivered. "Let me do this very small thing to repay you. Let me buy you a plane ticket so you can go shake the hell out of this cowboy of yours."

"It's not that easy." She shook her head, hoping to clear the heat that seemed to be hazing her good sense. Why else would she be feeling the insidious tug of temptation? "I don't know where he is."

"An investigator would locate him in a day."

"Maybe, but that'd be—" Underhanded. Over-the-top. "—wrong."

"Scared?"

She bristled at the low-voiced taunt. "Scared of what?"

"I don't know, Catriona," he said in that same low, dangerous voice. "Maybe you're scared of what you'll find out about your cowboy."

"Scared of the truth? No way."

"Then let me—"

"No," she said quickly, adamantly. "If you insist on repayment, you can buy me that dinner sometime."

"Think about it."

"Oh, I'm sure I will think about it." With a rueful half smile, Cat shook her head. She would think about it most every waking hour, and dream about it while she slept. "I'll think about it but I won't change my mind."

After he disconnected, Rafe's smile curled with the thrill of a challenge innocently laid down and not-so-innocently accepted. He didn't know how he would change her mind, only that he'd give it one hell of a shot. And not only because she'd challenged him, not only because his life had become too easy, too predictable, too dissatisfying.

He knew his brothers treated his part in their baby-making pact as a joke. *Rafe as a father? Shoot, he's too irresponsible, too reckless. Too shallow. He hasn't grown up himself.* Not that he blamed them for that opinion, since it amused him to overplay his reputation. Charm, after all, was the one and only thing he excelled at.

But now it was time to show his hand. Time to show his brothers that he was up to the challenge, that he could do something as well as—even better than—them.

For once he could give something back to his family.

He'd found the right woman, but could he find the means to change her mind?

Six

"What made you change your mind?"

Cat sighed, unleashing a fraction of the tight breath she swore had been backing up in her lungs for days. Ever since she left a message on the man at her side's voice mail to say, *I have changed my mind. I would like to accept your offer to help.* The man she'd found already seated when the flight attendant walked her through the curtain into first class on this Sydney to Los Angeles flight.

Clever, clever man. He knew she'd have balked at accepting a first-class ticket and his company, so he'd waited until the last minute to spring both on her.

Shaky already with nerves and an awful sense of what-have-I-gotten-myself-into, he hadn't helped matters by standing and kissing her shell-shocked lips. Nothing explicit, nothing extreme, just a brief taste of mint and a wicked lick of temptation that curled Cat's toes and weakened her knees. So much so that she'd slumped into her seat while he calmly explained about having some business to attend to. Thought he might as well travel with her. Make sure she found her cowboy, who he'd located recovering from injury in Vegas. Two birds with the one stone. Etc, etc.

How could she dispute what sounded too glib and convenient but could be the straight truth? He worked, apparently, as some kind of executive with Carlisle Hotels. He was, reputedly, a gambler. He could, easily, do business in Las Vegas.

With a small elite audience and a hovering flight attendant wanting to make her feel at home—in first class with champagne? not likely!—she couldn't kick up a fuss. And when she did open her mouth to question his motives, Rafe pressed a finger to her lips and suggested she follow the safety demonstration.

As if a whistle and light would do her any good if this big bird went down over the Pacific Ocean!

By then the plane was rolling and he was asking why she'd changed her mind and it was much too late to change it back again.

"My stepmother," she replied. "She changed it for me."

"I'm going to have to meet the wicked stepmother. Find out how she managed the impossible."

She turned her head and found him watching her, his eyes alight with the same smile that laced his voice. Silky and sexy and altogether too satisfied. As if he'd known she would change her mind, which he couldn't possibly have done since she hadn't known herself.

Not until after she'd dialed his number in a furious fit of pique, driven by one phone call from the step-monster. No one had the power to play her emotions like Pamela McConnell Smythe—not even Gordon Samuels, although he came close!

"She manages the impossible by being impossible," she told Rafe. "You do not want to meet her, believe me."

"Okay. But I would like to hear how she influenced your decision."

The jumbo had reached the runway and it lumbered in a slow arc to face east, the ocean, her future. Cat's heart started to thunder like a stampeding steer. Why not tell him? Talking might take her mind off the rising panic that threatened to engulf her—a turbulent anxiety that rivaled the high-pitched whining of jet engines impatient for takeoff.

"Pamela loves to tell me all about her daughters and their brilliantly successful careers." Compared to, say, her own spectacular struggle to survive. "And she can't resist reminding me, in subtle little ways, how much keeping Corroboree in the family meant to my father."

"And has she helped you to do that?"

"She offered once, but…" Cat shrugged instead of finishing the sentence. *But I chose to take Drew's money instead.* At the time it had seemed the better option. Better than accepting help from a woman who didn't think she could do the job, who undermined her confidence at every turn, who made her sweat with guilty, angsty fear over letting down her father.

"But…?" Rafe prompted.

The giant engines roared and he leaned across the console between their seats, ducking his head to wait for her answer. Expecting her to speak that answer close to his ear.

Cat stared. At the smooth curve of hair behind his ear and the bristly texture of his sideburn before it. At the squared edge of his jawbone and the flat plane of his cheek. She swallowed. Her fingers curved reflexively around the ends of the armrests, gripping tight, partly because the plane was accelerating down the tarmac and partly because her senses had been hijacked by wild imaginings.

Pressing her lips to that ear. Touching his skin. Biting the lobe.

His prompting question forgotten, she closed her eyes and held on tighter. Then his hand covered hers, enclosing it in heat and the surprise of his palm's texture. Not silky smooth like the rest of him, but slightly rough and very male.

She couldn't stop the sensual shudder that rose from deep

inside when the pressure of his hand increased, stroking over her knuckles and between her fingers. And when he leaned closer to say, "We'll be up there soon. Just hang on tight," she couldn't help the flare of her nostrils as she breathed deeply and caught the musky note of his scent.

Yes, she was slightly nervous of flying.

Yes, he was helping her overcome it—not with his reassuring words, but by guaranteeing she forgot all about the unlikely physics that kept 350 tons of metal airborne.

Did he know how violently he affected her?

Probably. She imagined all women responded the same way to his sexy sweet-talking appeal. God knows, the gossip magazines insinuated so. Not that Cat read them, as a rule, but in the last week she'd allowed her curiosity to type his name into an internet search engine. She'd allowed that curiosity to start reading from some of the sites unearthed…until she'd realized what she was doing and shut her computer down in self-disgust.

The plane lifted and her stomach took a lifetime to catch up. She eased her grip on the armrest but he didn't take his hand away until she wriggled and tugged. "I'm okay now."

And because he was looking at her too closely, his amazing eyes narrowed and fixed on her face, his expression speculative and ready to call her on that lie, she circled back to their interrupted conversation about her stepmother.

"Pamela withdrew her offer of help. She's just waiting for me to fail."

"Is that why you want to save your station so badly?"

"No, that's for my father and myself." The quiet intensity of her words resonated with the same vibrant power as the climbing jumbo for several seconds. Maybe longer. Then a touch of wryness curved Cat's lips. "Although I wouldn't knock back the chance to do something—just once—to wipe the floor with her patronizing attitude."

"I imagine that goes for Samuels, too."

"Crikey, yes! Doubly."

Settling back in the superwide seat, she allowed herself to image that scenario. For the short time it lasted, my, it was good, but then the raw reality of her situation shoved its ugly head into her fantasy. She had no clue how to resolve her mess. This trip to America was only to answer questions, to close her past with Drew, to arm herself with the truth before facing her future.

"I take it he's not looking after your place then, while you're away?"

Cat pulled a face. "Good guess. Bob and Jen Porter are feeding the animals and keeping an eye on things."

"Good neighbors."

"Yes." Her only good neighbors. Her only support. And not nearly enough in the long run.

Perhaps he saw the change in her expression because he leaned closer, his voice lowered to an intimate, conspiratorial level. "Whatever you're thinking, Shauna will be along in a minute to cure it."

Cat frowned. "Shauna?"

He indicated the flight attendant with a nod and a wink. The latter was for the sleek and beautiful Shauna. Figured that he knew her name already. Figured that he was flirting with her already. What didn't figure was Cat's own fierce reaction.

"How will she cure me?" she asked, testy with herself for what felt like the razor's slice of jealousy. She had no right to those feelings. No right to any feelings for Rafe Carlisle.

He turned her way again, just a slight roll of his head against the soft leather headrest and he was looking right into her eyes. Smiling right into her eyes. "She'll be along with champagne."

"The universal first-class cure-all?"

"I didn't know you were such a cynic."

"I'm a realist, Rafe, and this—" she waggled her hand, indicating everything around her in the first-class cabin, including him "—only happens in the movies. It's not real. Not in my life."

He raised a lazy eyebrow. And before she realized his purpose, he twined his fingers through hers and picked up her hand. Mesmerized by the soft stroke of his thumb across the center of her palm, by the unwitting intimacy of their linked fingers, by the flare of heat in her belly, Cat blinked slowly. She sat helplessly entranced while he stroked her knuckles against the soft leather of the seat. While he lifted them to brush his cheek and then to touch the sensual fullness of his bottom lip.

"See—" the warm breath of his word washed against her knuckles "—it is all real."

Crikey, he was lethal.

She was in trouble if he kept this up all the way to L.A.

She tugged her hand, and after a short tussle that brought heat to her cheeks, he let her reclaim it. He touched the back of his hand to her face and she jerked back, furious with herself for overreacting, but also with him for playing his games with her. Surely there had to be better in-flight entertainment.

"This is a long flight." She kept her voice and her gaze even, despite the furious heat in her cheeks. "Let's get a few things straight, so there are no mixed messages."

"I'm listening."

"I'm serious, Rafe. Please."

"So am I," he said, mimicking her stern tone. "What messages are getting mixed, Catriona?"

"I'm not a plaything," she said tightly. "Don't toy with me."

"Toy with you?"

"This…*thing*…you do with women."

"This…thing?"

She clicked her tongue with annoyance. Did he have to repeat everything she said in that pseudo-studious way? "Flirt. Kiss. Touch. The lines, the looks. We both know you don't mean it, so just cut it out!"

For a long moment he eyed her in a way she couldn't fathom. Then, with devastating slowness, he brushed his fingertips down the length of her hair. "I promise I won't toy with you, Catriona. But I can't promise not to touch you."

What was that supposed to mean? Cat's heart beat hard and high in her chest. She had to swallow before she could attempt to speak. "What if I don't want you to touch me?"

"Let's make a deal." His voice was low, lazy, lethal. "Just so there are no mixed messages."

Cat swallowed again.

"I won't touch you if you don't want me to. I won't do anything you don't want me to." He extended his hand. "Do we have a deal?"

Did they? Mouth dry, heart thumping, she stared at his hand a second, two, three, while she mulled over his terms. It sounded too good to be true.

"Well, Catriona?"

"My call? You'll back off whenever I say?"

"Promise."

They shook on that, just as Shauna appeared with the promised champagne. Cat settled back into her cushy seat and rubbed her fingers over the warmth lingering from his handshake while her trepidation remained, unallayed, unrelenting.

After all, hadn't a handshake deal with another charmer gotten her into this mess?

The investigator Rafe employed had found Drew Samuels easily enough, shacked up with a woman named Cherrie. He'd told Catriona about the injury but not about the woman. That's why he'd hung around outside the apartment complex after Catriona disappeared inside. That's why he was waiting when she came out half an hour later, ready to take her back to their hotel for some intensive play time.

Yes, he'd promised not to toy with her, but this wasn't that kind of play. This was about making her laugh and forget the ex and everything he'd done to hurt her. This was about treating her and indulging her and reminding her that she was a desirable woman.

Then he would get serious.

As for their deal…well, like all contracts, the devil was in the detail. As he'd told her on the plane, he couldn't agree to not touching but he could shake on not trying anything she didn't want. And Catriona did want him. He felt the spark when their gazes connected, the heat when their fingers meshed, the soft sexy tension when he brushed his mouth with her knuckles.

She might not have realized it yet, but she would.

Slowing with the traffic as they approached the Strip, he cut her a sideways look and felt the same gut kick of reaction as five minutes before, when she slid into the passenger seat of the rental sports car without a word. At worst he'd expected a short dose of cynicism on men in general; at best a fiery diatribe on the specific worm who'd sold her out without a breath of warning.

He hadn't counted on her looking so pale. So lost. So damn beaten.

He hadn't counted on his own savage response, either. If the bastard had had the common courtesy to walk her outside—hell, she hadn't known he was waiting, she'd told him to go and attend to his business, she'd catch a cab—Rafe would likely have given in to the violent need to grind his face in the dirt. That rocked him almost as much as Cat's silence. He wasn't a violent man. And he didn't even have the full story on Drew Samuels…although he intended to get it once they arrived back at their hotel and he could concentrate only on her, instead of the car and the traffic and the tourists who wandered around in a bright-lights-induced coma. Even though it was only midmorning.

They were half a block from their hotel when he changed his mind and kept on driving. It was a whim, but the kind that sat right in his gut and even righter in his mind the farther he drove without her taking any notice. When he pulled over to dispense with the convertible's roof, she finally sat up straighter and looked about. Behind her dark glasses he couldn't see her eyes, but he knew they roamed the red desert vista with dawning realization.

"Where are we? Where are we going?"

"Nowhere in particular. Just driving."

"For how long?" she asked after a moment.

"As long as it takes," Rafe answered easily as he steered the Jaguar back onto the single-lane road. Divergent currents of warm and cool air eddied through the car, whipping several long tresses around her face. "You might want to tie your hair back."

The powerful engine pleaded for release in a low rumbling purr he couldn't deny. He opened her up for the time it took to hit the speed limit—and a bit more—and she thanked him with a blood rush of sheer speed-induced pleasure. Not as good as sex, not as good as flying or outwitting a sharp opponent at the poker table, but the next best thing.

He glanced at Catriona. She'd given up holding her hair, and it sailed beyond the car's confines in wild cinnamon streamers that obscured her face. He hoped the rush of speed had chased away some of her anxiety, that the sparse landscape with its rich ochre shades and wild, rough edges would feel enough like home to ease her tight expression.

That's what he'd meant by "as long as it takes."

He turned up a dirt trail leading nowhere in particular and eased off the speed. He aimed to find somewhere to pull over, somewhere they wouldn't be disturbed. He hoped she was ready to let all that heartache pour out.

"Don't you need to get back? To your business?"

They'd been stopped out here—wherever that was—for a while. Cat didn't know how long. She'd walked until her sandals started to rub through her numbness and register as imminent blisters. Then she'd returned to the sleek silvery blue sports car and climbed back into her seat.

Rafe didn't move. "I don't have to be anywhere."

But despite the peace of this place and his relaxed immobility in the driver's seat—how could someone slouch so gracefully?—she couldn't sit still. She felt edgy and restless, as if the short walk had freed all her simmering frustrations from their previous frozen numbness.

She turned in her seat, better to face him. "Why did you bring me out here?"

"To walk. To talk if you want. I'm a good listener."

"Talk." She made a tight growling noise in her throat. "That won't help me any!"

"Would it help if you tossed rocks at something? There are some sturdy-looking cacti out here. If you feel so inclined."

No, she didn't feel like throwing things any more than talking. She felt like...like...

"Did you know about Cherrie?" Harsh, almost accusatory, the question exploded from deep inside, deep down where panic and anger and despair roiled in a churning cauldron of contained emotion.

"The girlfriend?"

"The *pregnant* girlfriend," she corrected, and she could see by Rafe's face that that much was news. And it struck her, randomly, inconsequentially, that he wouldn't be the only one stunned by the news. Her laugh came out low and bitter, and she shook her head slowly. "Can you imagine his father's face when he finds out?"

"Samuels doesn't want grandkids?"

"That's not the point. The point is Cherrie. Let's just say Gordon would welcome even *me* with open arms in preference to a Vegas showgirl-slash-waitress!"

She could feel him watching her, silent as the spread of desert landscape, intent as one of the hawks that circled over a distant canyon. "Was that ever an option? Samuels as your father-in-law?"

"I thought so. We lived together for a while, when Drew was home from rodeos. He and his father had a falling out, and we'd always been friends. It became…more. I took his money thinking we'd end up running Corroboree together, that we'd be partners, and the silly handshake I'll-pay-you-back deal was only about my pride." Now she'd started talking, the words simply wouldn't let up. It didn't matter who she was telling or whether he wanted to know, she just had to let it all out. "Why couldn't he have told me about Cherrie and the baby and his busted shoulder? I would have understood him needing the money. I could have done something without him selling me out to his father!"

God knows what, but something! For a start she would have avoided this pointless trip, saved herself the discovery of Drew's failure firsthand, of meeting the beaten flatness of his eyes. Of knowing he'd been too weak to return her calls and tell her the truth.

"I take it his rodeo dream didn't pan out?"

"He says he was doing all right until he got laid up with injury, but who knows? As far as I know he didn't even tell his father that much. Back home I kept hearing how well he was doing on the circuit." She slapped a hand against the console. "I should have known better. I had my doubts when I stopped seeing his name in the results on the Internet."

"You were hoping you were wrong."

With a rueful sigh, she slumped back in her seat. "Yeah. I was hoping."

"Valid," he suggested after a long beat of pause, "since you love him."

That statement, spoken quietly, evenly, stretched through the ensuing silence and wrapped around Cat's conscience. She frowned. Did she love Drew? Present tense…no, she didn't. Past tense…yes, she must have. Why else would she have trusted him? Why else would his betrayal have struck such an acute hurt in her heart?

Because *the result* mattered so deeply. Because, now, she would have to find some way to repay Samuels and she feared that selling at least part of Corroboree was her only option. She feared that Samuels wouldn't stop at part, that he would keep hammering away until he had the whole.

"He's always wanted Corroboree." A simple statement, but her voice ached with all that meant. Failing her father and failing herself. "I don't know what I'm going to do, Rafe."

She'd turned toward him, her arms spread in unconscious appeal, and although he didn't move a muscle, she sensed a change. A new alertness. As if he'd been sitting there waiting for her to get to this point. Waiting for his cue to take over.

"You're not going to do anything, Catriona. Not yet."

"But—"

"You're tired, you're stressed, you're emotional. That's not the time to be making big decisions."

True, but…

Rafe the listener, lounging back in his sports car seat, prompting her to toss her verbal rocks at the abandoned terrain…*that* Rafe she trusted. This intent, take-charge version disturbed her at some elemental level. Having to seek his advice on what to do next disturbed her even more, yet she couldn't help herself. She felt so lost and fretful she might as well have been out there, wandering across the red-tinged vastness of the Nevada landscape, alone and without a compass.

"When will I be ready?"

"Not before tomorrow," he said without pause. "At the earliest."

"And what do you suggest I do in the meantime?"

"You're in Vegas." Slowly he straightened out of his lazy sprawl. "I suggest twenty-four hours of self-indulgence."

Oh, right, sure. "You think I'm going to what…take in the

sights and a show? Check out a few casinos? When my world is falling apart?"

"I think you need to forget about your world for twenty-four hours."

"And experience yours?"

"Not so much mine. I'm talking spas and shopping. Relaxation and retail therapy."

"Not my thing."

"You're a woman." His gaze lingered on her lips. His mouth kicked with a hint of wicked knowledge. "Of course they're your thing."

"They're a waste of money."

"I've got plenty."

Exasperated by his attitude, she threw her hands in the air. "If you're so damn desperate to squander your money, why don't you spend it on something worthwhile?"

For a long second he eyed her silently. Then he smiled. "Oh, I intend to, baby."

Seven

Cat didn't so much give in as give up.

Physically tired, emotionally drained, she put herself into the hands of Bridget—who worked for the hotel in some do-whatever-the-wealthy-guest-wants capacity—because it was easier than convincing Rafe that she didn't go for the conventional female treats. That her idea of self-indulgence was sleeping in an extra hour on the odd Sunday morning and buying fresh peaches instead of canned. That the only spa she'd ever seen was in her stepmother's bathroom. That her idea of retail therapy would be unlimited credit at a stud cattle sale.

Bridget, it turned out, was very good at her job.

She had a way of drawing Cat into conversation and distracting her with an apparent keen interest in Australia and all things outback. Then, midconversation, while they strolled through the hotel's high-rent shopping arcade, she would point out something and get all excited.

"Oh, that would look smashing on you, Catriona! You must try it on!"

Cat's eyes boggled at the designer names—Dior, Chanel, Prada, Armani—and balked at the changing-room doors. Bridget cajoled. Cat gave in. Saleswomen gushed. And against all previous experience and knowledge of herself, she started to enjoy the trying-on, being-gushed-over thing.

The slinky fabrics shimmered against her skin when she moved. The world's cleverest push-'em-up bra produced never-seen-before cleavage. Cunningly shaped dresses defined her waist and skimmed her hips, and in the magical mirrors she looked tall and slender and sexy.

It was a deception, she knew, but a harmless one. A girly game she would soon forget back in the real world, but for now she conceded Rafe's point. Today she needed to forget that world. Just for a little while.

After the shops, she gave herself over to the day spa staff without demur. When they asked which treatments she preferred, she shrugged and smiled. "You decide for me. Just wake me when you're done." Several hours and one body wrap, one oxygenating facial, one hair revival treatment and one full makeup application later, she was done.

Strangely enough she wasn't done in.

On her way up to the top floor of their hotel, her heart hammered fifteen to the dozen with what felt like anticipation. Outside the door to their suite she paused and drew a deep breath and called herself to task for that ridiculous nervous excitement. She didn't even know if Rafe was in. She didn't know if she would see him at all tonight. One still-functioning kernel of her brain cynically suggested that this whole long afternoon of Cat-pampering served another purpose—it had taken her off his hands so he could do whatever he'd come to Vegas to do.

And what if that's you, Catriona? What if he's come to Vegas to—

No! She didn't let that wanton thought go any further. She didn't even know where it had come from, but it could go right back there! He hadn't even mentioned his need of a baby again, not once since that morning at Corroboree. For all she knew, he'd already found someone. For all she knew, he could be off finding someone now.

What if that someone is inside now? In this suite? In his bed?

"Then it's his business," she told herself sternly. Not hers to ponder or judge. Not hers to care about. She'd already made a fool of herself over their sleeping arrangements at check-in.

"A shared suite?" she'd objected. "Oh, no. I'll take an ordinary room."

Rafe's eyes had narrowed. "You expect me to pay for a room of your own? On top of the plane ticket? And the jet?"

He'd meant the private jet waiting in L.A., ready for the early-morning hop to Vegas. Another stunning surprise in a list that went on and on. "I'll pay for my own room," she'd said stiffly. "I'd rather have my own."

"Do you know what that will set you back?"

She'd guessed. He'd laughed. And the literal-minded clerk had corrected her miles-too-low assumption. Afterward, on their way to this penthouse suite, she'd paid more attention to the marble tiles and mother-of-pearl mosaics and intricate old-world furnishings.

"I didn't ask you to pay for my room," she said tightly, feeling gauche and ill equipped to deal with such plush surroundings. Feeling another swamping wave of what-have-I-let-myself-in-for panic.

Rafe had just shrugged with his trademark negligence. "It's a two-bedroom suite. I only need one."

They'd showered, changed, each on their separate side of the huge central living area. And she'd rushed through it all, dealing with her anxiety by focusing on what lay ahead with Drew.

Now, ten hours later, with her heart in her mouth, she forced herself to open the door and walk inside. Instantly she felt the empty silence and contradictory pangs of relief and disappointment.

She was alone.

"And that's okay, Cat," she told herself. She didn't need his company. She was used to alone...although not in such an alien habitat. She kicked off her sandals and prowled a circuit of the parlor. *The parlor. Huh.* That's what the concierge had called it when he'd shown them through. A grand name for a grand room in a grand suite of a grand hotel.

After picking up her sandals, which were making the place look untidy, she padded off to her bedroom. No need to feel abandoned. There was a television with about a zillion cable channels. Her choice of movies. She could get adventurous and order room service, which she would somehow pay for herself, and then—

She stopped short in the doorway to her bedroom.

Mouth open like a startled guppy, she stared at the boxes and bags—*shopping* bags—neatly stacked on the satin chaise beneath the picture window. It was not a small stack. Her stomach went into free fall.

Was it *everything* she'd tried on?

Heart palpitating, she slowly crossed the room. Had Rafe told Bridget to do this? To buy her all these things? Yes, he had plenty of money. He hadn't needed to tell her that. But she'd didn't want him wasting any more on her. She didn't need pretty clothes she would never wear.

Her breath caught as she opened the first box. It held the last dress she'd tried on. An evening dress she would never choose in a million years. White satin, tucked and pleated. Completely impractical.

She jammed the lid back on and kept her hands pressed down hard on the box. Not that she expected the dress to fling itself free like a jack-in-the-box. She didn't trust herself. If she didn't get rid of the thing—all the things!—right away, she might fall for the lure of that exquisitely soft fabric.

The temptation of playing dress-up again could strike her at a weak moment.

But not if she called Bridget—provided she was still on duty—to come and take it all away. She was pretty certain that once she'd eaten and slept and come to grips with the past twenty-four hours, she'd feel guilty enough about the cost of the spa treatments she couldn't give back. The clothes she could.

Pleased with that decision, she looked around for a phone...and heard the outer door to the suite open. Rafe. Her heart skipped and stalled, but for the life of her, she couldn't move. She was standing, frozen, midway between the chaise and the desk with the phone when he appeared in her doorway.

Their gazes met, linked, locked, and for a long moment that was it...no words, no movement, nothing but hot, heavy desire in her blood, in her breasts, in her belly. In the silent, sandalwood-tinted air of her bedroom.

Rafe moved first, his gaze ambling over her face, lingering on the soft-coral curve of her lips, taking in the carefully constructed wildness of her curls...and when he met her eyes again, Cat saw satisfaction and something else in those sea-green depths. Something that wasn't surprise. Something that electrified her sluggish nerves with wanton excitement.

If he'd said, *Take off your clothes,* Cat would have started stripping. It was that kind of look, that kind of response. That potent.

But all he said was, "Nice job," in that low, lazy way he had, and Cat felt a ridiculously sharp stab of disappointment. She hadn't really expected the let's-get-naked demand, but "You look good" would at least have given some credit to her. Instead he'd complimented the stylist.

"You paid them enough," she said. "You should expect better than a nice job."

His eyes narrowed a fraction. "Didn't you enjoy yourself? Don't you like your hair?"

"Do you?"

"Yeah," he said after a long beat of silence. Long enough for Cat to regret her hastily fired retort. Long enough for her heart to start thundering in her chest because his expression had changed, turned tricky and unreadable. "I like it. But then I liked it that night at your house, when you'd washed it and you smelled of peaches. I like it in that long braid that slaps against your spine when you walk. I liked it all mussed when you slept on the plane."

Crikey. She'd been looking for a your-hair-looks-good compliment. And he'd noticed all that!

"Right now you look like one of those Botticelli angels...but that's not the point. This afternoon was for your pleasure, Catriona, not mine."

For her pleasure, and she'd returned the favor by sniping about the cost.

Cat shook her head, a vain attempt to dislodge the scintillating effect of his comments. The knowledge that he'd watched her, noticed her, on all those occasions. A vain attempt to snap her brain into action.

"I did enjoy myself," she assured him finally. "Even the clothes."

A corner of his mouth quirked. "I wasn't sure how that part would go."

"I'm not a big fan of dressing up."

His eyes slid behind her, to the pile of bags and boxes. "Looks like you found something you liked."

"Oh, no. I mean, yes." Confused, she frowned. "Beautiful things, and fun to try on, and, yes, how could I not like them? But I don't want them. I can't keep them."

"Why not?"

"Because they're too expensive and I would never wear them." She lifted her arms and let them drop. "This is me—jeans and shirts. I don't go anywhere to wear flashy clothes."

"What about tonight?" he asked, ever so casually. She hadn't seen him move, but she noticed that he was lazing against the doorjamb. Posture as laidback as always, but those eyes still dangerously alert. Disturbingly sexy.

"What about tonight?" she asked warily.

"To thank me for today, for this afternoon, you're letting me take you to dinner."

Cat stared at him. Did he really think she would buy that excuse? She would have dinner with him…as a thank-you? What was wrong with that picture!

"You must be hungry."

"Yes," she conceded. She'd missed lunch. Breakfast on the plane seemed a lifetime ago. "I'm starving, actually. But I thought I'd just order in some room service and then crash."

"Even better. You want to eat formally at the table, or pizza while we watch a movie?"

The televisions were in the bedrooms and the next question went unasked, but she read it in the heat of his eyes as they flicked to her bed and back to her face.

Your room or mine?

Five minutes ago he'd looked at her and she'd almost started shedding clothes. Now he'd shaken her up enough for her brain to start operating on some subliminal level—enough to know that if she stayed in this suite, if they ordered in food, she would end up naked. She was too tired and too sensually smitten and too emotionally needy to resist.

And tomorrow she would hate herself.

"Well?" he prompted.

"I…I've changed my mind." Decision made, she spoke quickly, convincing that part of her that still wanted to stay in and get naked as much as convincing Rafe. "I'm in Vegas and I'll probably never be here again. I would like to go out— for a little while—to have a meal and see the lights and the famous fire-and-water show. Bridget said I shouldn't miss that! And I have to put at least one coin through the slots."

"You are in Vegas," he agreed, sounding not the least put out by her vacillations.

In fact, he looked a little too pleased with himself as he straightened from the doorjamb and came into her room. Cat stiffened reflexively. "What are you doing?"

"Choosing something for you to wear."

"You can't."

"I am."

He unlidded the top box. And stilled. Slowly, softly, he ran the back of his hand across the white satin, and Cat's skin tingled with heat as if he'd touched her in that same way. As he *had* touched her, on the plane.

When he started to lift the dress from the box, she stopped him with a hand on his arm. On the hard curved muscle of his forearm. "Not that one."

Slowly he lifted his gaze to hers. "Why not this one?"

"It's too formal." She took her hand back. "Too much."

"Are you going to find a complaint with every one of these?" he asked, reaching for a smaller bag.

It was the underwear—the lace and satin and gel cups and g-strings—she just knew it. Fighting the urge to grab and wrestle him for possession, she stood calm and still. "No. There's a green dress I tried on. It's probably in one of these bags. I'll wear that one."

"Green?"

"Sort of green." And sort of flattering, she remembered, the way the sheer layers of fabric draped from the halter neck over her breasts, and flared from the waist to an uneven hemline that played peek-a-boo with her knees.

Sort of sexy in a subtle way.

He smiled in a way that was definitely sexy—no "sort of" about it—as he handed over the underwear. As he told her to wear that dress because, "Sort of green's my favorite color."

Rafe didn't really have a favorite color. Not until he saw Catriona in that dress. It wasn't "sort of" green; it was knock-your-eyes-out, kick-in-the-gut, heart-pumping green.

Although that reaction, when she came out of her room fifteen minutes later, probably had as much to do with the shy heat in her eyes and the nervous jump of her pulse and the certainty that he'd be peeling that green lick of silk from her body in a couple of hours' time.

He'd thought about making that sooner. He was pretty sure he could have talked her into staying in, but then he'd have missed the awed delight in her wide eyes as they watched the water fountains play under golden lights. He'd have missed pouring her a glass of champagne and feeding her her first taste of truffles…and watching her spit them back out again. He'd have missed the quiet intensity of her gaze on his face while he told her about his apartment in Sydney, her husky laughter at his collection of hotel management war stories, the gusty appetite with which she consumed her meal.

And, yeah, he'd have missed *this* moment.

Defeated by her white-chocolate and raspberry dessert, she'd finally laid down spoon and fork and sighed with dreamy completion. And, yeah, he'd been watching her play with the stem of her champagne flute and thinking about another kind of completion, when she'd looked up at him and smiled. "How did you know this is what I needed?"

"Cheesecake?" he'd asked. "Or more champagne?"

"You know what I mean. Tonight. This afternoon. Everything. You've taken my mind off my problems, as you promised, and you've made me laugh when I thought I'd never laugh again. I haven't thanked you."

"I think you just did."

She studied him a moment, her eyes solemn. Her expression serious. "Just saying thank you seems inadequate."

"I'm enjoying your company."

"Me, too." Her smile flashed, soft and sincere. "This morning you said you were a good listener. You're not so bad in the talking field, either."

"I'm not just a pretty face."

"No." Their eyes met and her eyes flamed as if she, too, was thinking of other things. Other areas of expertise.

"You ready to find out what else I'm good at?" he asked slowly.

The pulse in her throat fluttered. Her smile faltered and her laugh sounded brittle and edgy with nerves. "Oh, I don't know that I'll ever be ready for that."

"No? There's an old saying my father liked to use." He stood and held out his hand, daring her to take it. Daring her to trust him. "Fortune favors the brave."

He didn't take her back to their suite, as Cat had anticipated when his fingers wrapped hers in the promise of startling heat and solid purpose. He took her by the hand and led her to the casino—not to one of the high-rollers' rooms with the other rich and famous and beautiful, but to the main floor and the endless raft of slot machines. Indulging her. Then rattling her by standing at her back and offering instruction close to her ear. Resting a casual hand on her shoulder. Engulfing the bare stretch of her back in the heat of his body.

She couldn't concentrate on the mindless roll of symbols and pictures before her eyes. Not when her body wanted nothing else but to turn and press hard against him. To bite his ear and say: *Enough. Let's go back to our room and see what you're really good at.*

It was better when the machine chomped her last credit and they moved to the roulette wheel…although that might have been due to their astonishing run of luck. Excited by the rattle of the wheel and the rush of color and the adrenaline hit when the ball dropped, she didn't even blink when he turned and pressed a kiss to her lips.

When he grinned and said, "Our luck's running hot, baby," she smiled right back.

"Must be the green dress."

"Nah," he drawled. "It's you."

If only it were, she thought, before she could stop herself. Then she excused herself that moment of whimsical dreaming by blaming the champagne and the touch of his hand on her back and the whole fantastical nature of this day.

A day out of time. A day out of reality. A day that would never be repeated.

Their number came up again and she laughed with a giddy lack of restraint at the pile of chips the croupier pushed their way. Except, at the end her laugh evolved into a giant yawn. Rafe, of course, noticed.

"You want to call it a night?" he asked.

Her stomach tightened, her pulse jittered, but she met his gaze with a reckless sense of what will be, will be. "I think I probably should before I pass out and you have to carry me home."

"Now that sounds like fun."

He put his arm around her as if he might actually follow through, and Cat panicked at the inglorious thought of him trying...and stumbling because she weighed more than this sexy green dress let on. "If you're carrying me," she said quickly, breathlessly, "then who's going to carry all our winnings?"

"You won it. You get to carry it."

"Me?" Cat shook her head. "Oh, no, I didn't. This is all yours."

"No," he said easily. "This night's all yours."

Stunned, head spinning faster and louder than the roulette wheel at their back, she stared into his face. He looked serious. He looked like he meant it. "I can't. You can't. No way."

"Think about it, Catriona. It's a lot of money. In your situation—"

"It's *your* money!"

Their eyes connected, clashed, and his flared with some kind of challenge. "Okay," he said softly. "Let's make this interesting."

Everything inside her tensed, stilled, focused on that dangerous glint in his eyes. "Interesting?"

"Let's up the ante."

Cat had to swallow and moisten her Nevada-dry mouth before she could get her throat and mouth to cooperate. "What do you propose?"

"One last spin. Red or black. All or nothing. If you win, you keep all the money. Enough to pay off your debts and some to spare."

"And if I lose?" Cat's voice was barely a whisper.

"You marry me. You have my baby. And I pay off your debts."

Eight

Afterward, Cat couldn't believe that she'd accepted such a crazy fantastical wager. That she'd calmly pushed all their chips onto black, before standing at the center of a hushed crowd watching the wheel spin and the numbers whirl and the colors slow from a gyrating blur to a distinguishable red-black-red-black sequence.

She hadn't thought he meant it. She hadn't believed he would go through with it. But then, she hadn't known that a person—two people, actually—could stroll right into the Marriage License Bureau and fill out the necessary paperwork for a wedding.

Little more than an hour after the fateful ball rattled to its resting place on red seven, she found herself married to the man at her side.

Rafferty Keane Carlisle. She hadn't even known his full name until they applied for that license. He was a virtual stranger, and he was her husband.

Somewhere between the wedding chapel and the hotel lobby, the molasses-thick stupor in Cat's mind stopped swirling long enough to let that detail seep in, along with all its ramifications. At the roulette table tonight, she'd won herself a husband. A rich husband who would pay off her debts so she could keep Corroboree.

A husband who wanted a baby conceived as soon as possible.

That particular ramification ambushed her completely as the elevator doors slid noiselessly shut, and the mirror-lined cubicle commenced its smooth ascent. Earlier she'd thought about sleeping with him, at least a dozen times during dinner alone. She'd decided that this night would probably end in his bed, but that had been part of the whole fantasy twenty-four hours. Part of the makeover, of licking her wounds, of rebounding from the Drew debacle and reasserting herself as a woman. Something to regret in the morning, and to walk away from once she returned to the real world.

But during that adrenaline- and champagne- and lust-fueled casino madness, she'd allowed fantasy and reality to collide. To connect. To join and meld and bond.

A wave of heat shadowed that thought. A rippling montage of bodies joining and melding and bonding in a tangle of Egyptian cotton sheets. She felt the heat in her cheeks and her eyes and the softened fullness of her lips, and she let her head drop a little, away from the telltale evidence in the mirror before her.

From the corner of her eye she could see his right hand tapping a lazy beat against the elevator wall, and she remembered the soft brush of those fingers in a dozen places, a dozen times. She remembered, and her pulse began to drum in time with his fingers.

Unable to watch any longer—not without taking that hand and drawing it to the achy heat of her body—she lifted her head and let it roll back against the cool, mirrored wall. For a second she closed her eyes and attempted to block out that insistent beat of desire with the image of their left hands joined by the celebrant. Left hands wearing the plain gold bands borrowed from the hotel concierge and about as disconnected from reality as this whole surreal night.

But that carefully constructed mental image faded, replaced by another. His hand drawing her into his body. His face blurring in and out of her dazed focus as he bent and pressed his lips to hers. *Go ahead and kiss the bride, now.* Heat washed through her veins, pooled sweet and liquid, low in her body.

She needed to think. They needed to talk before this went any further. Before this sexual energy took total possession of her mind as well as her body.

Restless, she rolled her shoulders. Shifted her feet. Their upper arms bumped and parted in what should have been a casual brush of contact, except it charged Cat with enough power to light up the whole Vegas strip.

Her eyes jolted open. A low, needy sound growled up from her throat. At first she thought it was in her mind, her own silent howl of protest because that one grazing brush of his jacket against her bare skin left her baying for more. But then their eyes met in the mirror with a hot, electric force that rocked her to her toes.

Oh, yes, she had groaned out loud. That knowledge was in his hot stare. It tugged tight in her belly and ached in her breasts.

Oh, yes, she wanted him. But somehow she'd imagined falling into bed with the Rafe from tonight's dinner, from the long conversations during their night on the plane, from the breakfast table at Corroboree. The man who'd lounged naked in her guest-room bathroom without batting an eyelid. The flirt with the knowing smile and the drawled lines that made her laugh or roll her eyes or fire back a cynical retort.

The man in the mirror was not that Rafe.

His eyes burned with a fierce flame. The lines of his classically hewn face were set with an intensity that both thrilled and terrified her.

And it struck her, in that long, drawn-out moment, that he'd barely spoken a word since that fateful moment in the casino. Nothing beyond the necessary instructions, as he took over and swept her along with an efficiency and purpose she'd not seen in him before. Up until now she'd been too dazed, too shocked, too brain-sluggish to work that all out.

Her heart beat slow and heavy in her chest. Pounding with the knowledge that she'd underestimated Rafe Carlisle. Pounding with the fear that she'd bitten off way more than she could chew.

The elevator chimed their floor, a brief rich peal that barely impacted on the tension inside the car. The tension inside Cat. "We're here," she said, surprising herself with the calm clarity of her voice. Yet she couldn't coax her limbs to move or force her gaze to disconnect from his.

"Finally."

And that one quietly uttered word propelled Rafe into action. Before she realized his purpose, he'd turned and ducked one arm under her thighs to swing her into his arms.

Her eyes widened as he carted her out of the elevator. "No, you can't. I'm too—"

"Too what, Mrs. Carlisle?" He stopped and met her startled eyes with a look of grim satisfaction.

Crikey. Mrs. Carlisle. That was her!

That whammy effectively wiped her mind clean of whatever she'd been about to say and a good lot else besides. He started striding toward their suite, and the combination of that motion and the wall of his body hard against hers joggled Cat's senses back to life.

She wrapped her arms around his neck and held on tight.

Her dangling legs brushed his hip and thigh, curling her toes with raw heat. One of her sexy new shoes fell from her arched foot, and she almost told him to leave it be. But he turned and dropped down on his haunches so quickly that her world tilted and spun.

"Put me down. I'm too heavy," she gasped as he came back up again, one delicate, glittery stiletto dangling from his hand. "You don't have to carry me."

"Yeah, I do. I have to carry you over the threshold. It's a tradition."

"I thought you said Alex was the old-fashioned one in your family. Since when have you worried about tradition?"

"Since I decided to marry you."

She huffed out a dubious breath. "So, about an hour, give or take? That hardly makes you an expert."

"An hour? What gives you that impression?" Stopped at the door to their suite, he looked long and hard into her eyes. "I made up my mind about you last week, baby. This wasn't a spur-of-the-moment decision."

Too much information? Admitted too soon?

As he extricated the key card from her itsy little nothing of a purse, Rafe suffered a moment's unease. She'd gone silent again, and he felt the stiffness of her body—a far different kind from his—against his chest and arms. Even through the intense buzz of arousal, he swore he could hear her mind ticking with questions. If he gave her half a chance, she'd launch a debate on the logic of what they'd just done. If he didn't keep her occupied, she might try to wangle another crazy handshake deal with him.

He wasn't about to give her *half* of half a chance. And once he got her inside, he intended to keep her very occupied.

The door swung open and he angled her through, swinging her with enough velocity that she gasped and caught hard at his shoulders and neck. Yeah, he liked the clutch of her fingers. The puff of her breath against his skin. But mostly he'd wanted to distract her from that thinking. From voicing the question he'd seen forming on her lush lips.

"I'm too big for this rubbish," she reprimanded. "You're lucky you haven't done yourself an injury!"

"Yeah, well, I've always considered myself a lucky bastard." He stopped spinning her and looked into her eyes. "And I've been particularly lucky with you."

Her eyes narrowed. "That roulette bet was only even money. A fifty-fifty chance, either way."

"True, but that's not what I meant." Luck had been on his side from the moment that storm sent him Catriona's way, and he'd caught one lucky break after another ever since. Her changing her mind. Finding the cowboy in Vegas. His impulsive challenge to up the ante.

"Then…what? And what did you mean about this not being spur-of-the-moment?"

Ignoring her questions, he started moving again, carrying her through the sitting room toward her bedroom.

"Stop." She pushed at his chest. "Put me down. We have to talk about this."

"Yeah, we do and we will. But not now. This is my wedding night, and the only thing I'm interested in discussing is how we're going to spend it." At the door he stopped and looked into her face. "And where. Is your bedroom okay or would you prefer we went to mine?"

Stunned eyes stared back into his.

"Yours, then." He nudged her door open with his shoulder. "I've been fantasizing about undressing you in this room all night."

He heard the soft explosion of her breath. "You didn't have to marry me to do that!"

Holding her tighter, he looked into her eyes and smiled. "I know. That's not why I married you."

"Then why did you?"

"Because you're going to be the mother of my baby."

The shock of that line registered deep in her eyes and resounded deep in Rafe's gut. The baby he'd only thought about

as his mother's grandchild had tonight taken shape and sub-
stance. A baby with Catriona's changeling eyes and calm
strength and solid values.

"How can you say that?" She began to struggle again, this
time with more determination. "I might not be able to get
pregnant. I might not be able to carry a baby. Did you think
about that?"

"I'm prepared to take my chances."

"Do you even *know* what those chances are?"

"Is there a reason you ask?" He carried her to the bed. Sat
with her in his arms. "Something in your history I should
know about?"

"No."

"Are you on any form of contraception?"

"No."

"Then why bring it up?"

All uptight and irritated, she clicked her tongue. "To illus-
trate why this was such a dumb idea!"

"You get your debts paid off. How is that dumb?"

"From *your* point of view. Marrying me doesn't ensure
you get this baby you need." Agitated, she started to wiggle
in his lap, trying to extricate herself from his arms. "I don't
understand why you had to go and marry me! I would have
slept with you without a marriage license. I know that. You
know that."

"Do I?" he asked evenly. "Because the way you're trying
to get away from me isn't exactly filling me with confidence."

Somehow, in her struggles, she'd managed to wiggle her
hip hard against him. She went still, and he watched her expression change from flushed annoyance to flushed knowledge. Watched her eyes flash with heat and spirit. "From
where I'm sitting you feel pretty damn full of confidence!"

"Him? Yeah, well, he's always confident."

"Yeah, well, I guess he has reason," she fired right back.
"With all your talk of wedding night expectations!"

She was really something, his wife. Sharp, smart, straight. And from where he sat, Rafe could see a choice of two options. Kiss her into submission—his first and favorite option. Or give her a better explanation of his motivation… before kissing her into submission.

Readjusting her to a more comfortable—and less distracting—listening position, he sighed resignedly.

"Say we'd walked away from that wheel tonight. Say we'd come back here and I'd got very lucky and talked my way out of that handshake agreement." Her eyes widened as if she'd forgotten about the deal they'd struck on the plane. "Say I'd managed to talk you into letting me touch you, any way I wanted to, every way I wanted to. Say you'd stripped out of that sexy little dress and invited me into your bed and your body."

She swallowed. Rafe's gaze dropped to that convulsive movement and saw the flutter of pulse in her throat. Satisfaction beat hard in his blood as his gaze returned to hers.

"Would you have still felt the same when the champagne wore off? Would you have woken up beside me in the morning? Would you have stuck around long enough to make this baby I need?"

She didn't answer, but then she didn't have to. Rafe knew a one-night stand would not sit right with a woman like Catriona, not the morning after. Nor would the kind of affair that consisted of baby-sex without any commitment.

"That's why I married you, Catriona. To make a baby." Slowly, gently, he palmed the curve of her stomach where that baby might one day grow. Felt the soft shiver of reaction in her flesh and saw it reflected in her eyes. "To do it right."

"You can't know I'm the right woman." That same shiver roughened the edges of her voice. "You don't know me. I don't know you."

"What do you want to know?"

"I don't know. Something. Anything. I didn't even know your full name." Rattled, edgy, her words came out in a rush. "I thought it might be Rafael."

"I'm Rafferty after my Gaelic grandfather—my mother's father. My brother Alex couldn't get the whole mouthful out when he was a tot, so he shortened it to Rafe. It stuck."

"See? I didn't know that. The Gaelic thing, I mean. You look Mediterranean."

"Courtesy of my birth father," he said shortly. He didn't share his background with many people, but Catriona had a right to know. This much at least. "My mother's Irish, though. Her name was Maura Keane."

"Your second name," she said softly. And that was enough, Rafe decided. Time to change the subject. He stroked the length of her arm, up and down, then paused at her shoulder. Touching the fabric of her dress with one fingertip. "My favorite color is green."

Her breath hitched when, with that one fingertip, he traced the draping folds of fabric down to her breast. He stopped. Leaned closer and sniffed the warm scent at her throat.

"My favorite scent is you."

She laughed, a husky sound of surprise that smoked through his blood and settled in his groin. "Whatever I smell like isn't me. It's a fancy day spa. It's lotions and potions."

Nuzzling closer, he inhaled again, then leaned back and met her eyes. "No, that's you...wife."

Her eyes darkened dramatically, and Rafe smiled with a satisfaction just as deep, just as dark, just as dramatic.

"My turn to find out about you," he said. "What's the origin of your name, Catriona?"

"I don't know."

"Okay...so, what's your favorite color?"

"I don't have one."

"Yeah, you do. Come on, own up."

"Sunset," she relented, after a short pause. "Pink and orange and indigo all strung together in a perfect outback sunset."

"Favorite scent?"

"Peaches. Fresh picked, ripe, juicy. We used to—" She

stopped suddenly, gave a dismissive shrug of one shoulder. "Just…peaches."

Rafe pressed his lips to that shoulder. Smooth. Warm. Sweet as a fresh-picked peach. "Come on," he coaxed. "You used to…?"

"We had an orchard. At Corroboree."

He remembered. An orchard that was now a graveyard of gray-timber and naked boughs. "And…?"

"If it didn't rain we didn't get fruit, but when we did…" She sighed, a soft sensual memory as her mouth curved into a smile. "You know when you take that first bite and the juice oozes out between your fingers and sweetness fills your nostrils…? That's my favorite scent."

Rafe kissed her then, while her eyes were soft and dreamy, while her lips were parted and curved with the contemplation of sweet and succulent fruit. Face cupped between his hands, his thumbs stroked the warm silk of her cheeks and along her jaw. He kissed her slowly, thoroughly, savoring the thought of peach juice on her lips, her tongue, her skin.

Gently he nipped at her bottom lip, and she opened to him with a sigh, a yielding that hummed in his throat with satisfaction. He licked into her mouth and felt a tremor run through her body. Hunger gripped his, not raw and primal like in the elevator, but rich and earthy and unexpectedly sweet.

Like the fruit she'd described; like Catriona, the woman. His wife.

Her arms settled heavily on his shoulders; the tips of her fingers traced a slow pattern against the back of his neck. And when he changed the angle of the kiss, she shifted in his lap, angling closer to his body. Pressing more firmly against his arousal while she kissed him back with her eyes fixed on his with drowsy-eyed passion.

And when he eased back slightly, drawing out of that long, lazy, kiss, she followed. Kissing the corners of his mouth. His chin. The line of his jaw. While her hands shaped his face and sifted through his hair.

Rafe laughed softly. Shook his head a little.

"What?" she breathed, hot against his skin. Hot against his thighs and areas in between.

"You."

"What about me?"

"I didn't expect you to be so…" He hesitated over word choice.

"Easy?"

"Willing," he corrected.

"Oh, I think you knew I'd be willing before we left this room tonight. You knew when I first suggested we stay in."

"Yet you decided to go out. Were you being contrary or cautious?"

She smiled, slow, sexy, mysterious. "What do you think?"

"I think I married a phony." Narrow-eyed he looked at her a second and then he gathered up her hair, masses of curls that he fisted in one hand. "I thought I'd have to work extrahard." With his free hand he started to undo the halter neck of her dress. "That I'd have to take this real slow."

"And?"

The question came out on a husk of breath as the last button came undone. As the fabric slipped from Cat's neck.

"And I don't know if slow is going to work." His fingers gathered the material, stroked it over her breasts, briefly teased her taut nipples, then were gone. The dress pooled at her waist. His eyes met hers. Flames licked and burned. "What do you like, wife? Fast or slow?"

Cat's heart beat hard, knocking her ribs with the same deep sultry note as his voice. He demonstrated *slow* with the backs of his fingers, barely grazing her skin as they trailed upward over her ribs. She sucked in a breath, closed her eyes and waited, breath held, waited and willed him to keep going. To touch the breasts that grew tight and heavy with longing.

He didn't.

Those taunting fingers trailed back down to her waist. "That isn't slow," she groaned. "That's torture."

But when she opened her eyes, his were fixed on her breasts, on that artfully created cleavage that fleshed over the half cups of sheer white fabric. Heat traced the line of his cheekbones. Heat burned in the eyes he slowly raised to hers. His hands palmed her ribs, pressed up against the undersides of her aching breasts. "You prefer fast?"

"I prefer…efficiency. I don't like wasting time."

"Some things are meant to take longer." A slow finger traced the line where lace met flesh. "To draw out the pleasure."

Cat wasn't sure how much more drawing out she could stand. Or how much of Rafe Carlisle's expert brand of pleasure. For a hint of a second she revisited that moment in the elevator, that stab of fear, of knowing she'd bitten off more than she could chew.

But then his thumbs stroked over her nipples, and the spear of desire low in her belly and hot between her legs razed everything from her brain. Her breath hitched and caught as his head dipped and he brushed his whisker-rough cheek against the flesh that pushed out of her bra. That same breath rushed from her lungs in a long, low sound of wanting as he turned his head and kissed her sensitized flesh.

With his lips, with his tongue, with his teeth.

He laved her nipple through the sheer material of her bra, and she was so lost in the intensity of sensation, she didn't notice his hands at her back. Didn't register the clever flick of his fingers until the hooks she'd taken minutes to fasten gave effortlessly. Through the sensual pall that expertise vaguely registered. A dull glimmer of unease because he'd undone more kinds of bras that she'd ever seen.

But then his hands palmed her naked breasts and he made a guttural sound of arousal that echoed through her whole body.

With single-minded concentration, he circled each nipple

with his fingertips. Played the aching tips with the pad of his thumb. Then with a soft grunt that was unabashedly male, unashamedly turned on, he lowered his head and sucked her deep into his mouth.

And, oh, man, he was just as skillful with his tongue on her nipples as when he'd kissed her mouth. Just as attentive. Just as big a tease.

She couldn't sit still. She couldn't stand her lack of participation. Fingers twined in his hair, she dragged his head away and up and their mouths met at exactly the right angle, with moist heat and erotic promise. They kissed, strong and hot and bold, and her body took on the rhythm of his mouth, the rhythm of sex.

It wasn't enough.

Without breaking the hot, wet contact of mouths and lips and tongues, she leaned her hands and her weight on his shoulders while she rose from his lap and resettled herself straddling his hard thighs. Their mouths parted but their gazes locked and held as his hands cupped her hips, molded her bottom and rocked her, slowly, deliberately, against the thick bulge of his erection.

"One of us is wearing too many clothes."

He leaned forward and blew warm air over her exposed nipples. "I gather that's not you."

For a second she could do nothing but ride the intense wave of pleasure generated at both breasts and her female core. Then she wiggled back a few inches.

"Quick on the uptake," she murmured, "for one so slow on the uptake."

"Are you complaining?"

"Maybe." With deliberate purpose she shifted her hands from his shoulders to his chest. Started unbuttoning his shirt. "Be warned. I'm all about efficiency."

"You don't want my help, then?"

"No." She finished the buttons, then looked into his eyes

as she tugged the shirt free of his trousers. "You are altogether too slow."

His laugh was thick and turned on. "You are altogether too sexy."

Cat pushed both his jacket and shirt from his shoulders. "You find my efficiency sexy?"

The last word hitched and hissed as he slid his hands under her dress and palmed her thighs. "I'm finding pretty much everything about you sexy, wife."

Oh, she loved how he said that. *Wife.* The word drummed in her blood as his thumbs stroked a sinuous path up her inner thighs. Built to a sweet pressure point of pleasure when he touched her through her panties.

He knew how to scintillate her with a word or a touch. He knew every sweet, delicious secret of a woman's body. He knew every smooth ego-seducing line.

And Cat knew why. He was Rafe Carlisle. Prince of the bedroom.

She held no illusions about what he was doing here on her bed, sliding the dress up her body, urging her to lift her arms so he could pull it all the way free. She was his wife—perhaps because he'd been born of a single mother, perhaps for his mother's sake—but only because it suited him. For as long as it suited him.

He tossed the dress behind her, on the floor, and she felt a sharp frisson of foreboding.

"That's a very expensive dress to treat so carelessly."

"I bought it," he told her. Hands spanning her waist. Head dipping to her breasts again. "I can treat it however I want."

And me? she wanted to ask. *Now you've bought me, will you treat me the same? Discard me as easily?*

But then his mouth closed over her nipple, and her back arched with a pull of desire that obliterated her disquiet. As she took pleasure from his expertise, as he rolled her from his lap onto the bed and slid her panties down her legs, she refused to think about how he'd grown so clever. How he knew exactly how to touch her, how long to tease her, how to use his tongue so ruthlessly.

When that clever tongue brought her to an abrupt, unexpected climax, he smiled with supreme masculine pride. "Nice, but too fast."

"Efficient," she retorted, her voice thick and slumberous, as she sagged back onto the bed. "Sufficient."

"Hardly." He finished undressing himself, and she prolonged her pleasure by watching. He let her. He stood before her, as spectacularly beautiful as she remembered from that morning in her guest room.

More so, with his assets at full look-at-me attention.

"I have condoms if you want."

She rolled her gaze from belly height to his face. Found his eyes narrowed and his eyes glittering with blatant arousal. Cat blinked, trying to gather her wits. "Condoms?"

"Protection. I've always used them. *Always*. But I had tests when this clause came up. For your reassurance."

"You had tests." To reassure *her* about unprotected sex. She frowned. "What about me?"

"Need I worry?"

"I've only had one lover." Drew, who was paranoid about an unexpected pregnancy screwing with his plans to make world champion. Maybe he'd had a premonition of what lay ahead. "He used condoms. He did with me, leastways."

And maybe this wasn't the time to be making cracks about Drew and the baby he clearly hadn't planned on making with his new girlfriend. Not the time to recall how much it had hurt, seeing the man you thought you loved, whom you wanted to spend the rest of your life with, shudder with dread at the thought of getting you pregnant.

Rafe still hadn't moved. His expression was guarded. His voice quiet and deliberate when he asked, "So, Catriona." Not *wife*, but *Catriona*. "Do we start now?"

Cat's stomach lurched as their gazes locked. "Perhaps you should have asked before we signed that marriage license."

"When you signed it," he said, "I took it as your binding word."

Not just that she would marry him, but that she would try to conceive his baby. Her heart thundered. Her world spun on its axis with the enormity of what she had done. And all she hadn't considered.

"Well, Catriona?"

A baby in return for saving Corroboree. Rafe's baby, yes, but also hers. A McConnell to carry on her family tradition, as her father had wanted. As she silently promised him, every time she stood at his grave, every time she stood under the unforgiving western sky and faced another tough season, another year of uncertainty.

She exhaled slowly, and her heart steadied to a dull, thick beat.

"Okay," she said finally. Then stronger, echoing the beat of her heart. "Yes. We start now."

Nine

Rafe knelt on the mattress beside the sexy sprawl of her naked body. "Are you sure, Catriona?"

She took a long time to answer. A long time while he took in the spill of her hair and the loose abandonment of her limbs. A hellishly long time with the scent of her desire in his senses and her eyes fixed low and still on his body.

Impatience growled through his blood, but Rafe waited.

He'd played on her vulnerabilities when he challenged her with the wager. He'd crowded her when she needed time to think, coerced her with the win-win nature of the deal, coaxed her with all she stood to win even if she lost that last spin. And then he'd rushed her to the altar before her head stopped spinning.

Suddenly he couldn't rush her any further. He wanted her willing now and tomorrow and the next day back home in Sydney. He wanted her willing for as long as he wanted her, however long that might be.

"You know there's no going back."

Her lids fluttered for an instant as if his words had scraped a nerve. But her redirected gaze met his with the openness that had attracted him to her from the very start. No coyness, no chicanery, just Catriona about to tell it like it was. "I said yes to not using a condom. That doesn't mean I'll fall pregnant. That's not something you or I can control."

"Is this a good time?"

"We're both naked." Her gaze slid back to the part of him that wasn't used to being naked in this situation. "I'd say that makes it as good a time as any."

Rafe laughed, short and gruff, as he stretched out beside her on the rich cream sheets. His knee brushed against the side of her thigh, accidentally the first time. Deliberately the second. He propped himself on an elbow so he could look down into her face. "I meant a good time in your cycle. For conception."

Her nostrils flared and her eyes darkened and jittered. Rafe felt it, too—the slam of reaction that was more than lust. Unsettling, unusual, uncomfortable.

"I'm not sure. Maybe." She shifted restlessly. One hand lifted, then dropped back against the bed. "I hate talking about this. I feel…"

Her voice trailed off as if she couldn't find the right word. Rafe sympathized. Easy to describe the hard tension in his groin. Not so easy to identify the weight bearing down on his chest.

"Can we forget about the conception part?" Direct as always, but her voice sounded raw and edgy. "Can we just do this?"

Now was the time to grin and tease her. To regain that sexy byplay of before by framing some lazy comeback about how he never "just did it." Except the smile wasn't happening and the line sounded superficial and shallow—the kind he'd drag up in any situation, for any woman.

This wasn't any woman. This was his wife gazing up at him, moistening her lips with apprehension. His wife whose hand shifted nervously against the sheet at his side.

And suddenly, intensely, he wanted those eyes, those lips, those hands on him.

"I think we'll get to that," he said slowly, heart drumming in his ears, desire throbbing in his blood. "But first I'd like you to touch me."

"Where?"

"Wherever you want."

She swallowed. "How?"

"That depends on where." Leaning closer he blew softly against her breast. A shiver of reaction rippled through her skin, traveled the length of her arm until her fingers curled into her palm. "Some places require a whisper." He leaned down and licked the skin at the inside of her elbow. Heard the change in her breathing. "Others demand a kiss." Lower still, he stroked the length of her thigh until her toes curled and her feet flexed. "And some require a firm hand." He continued that long, slow, firm caress all the way back up her body until he was gazing into her eyes.

Dark, turned on, not apprehensive anymore.

Satisfaction, fierce and intense, gripped Rafe where he lived. He watched her ease up onto her elbows to blow a whisper of sultry breath against his lips. Watched her follow him down to the mattress so she could press her tongue to his nipple.

"How am I doing so far?" she asked.

"Very efficient. Very—" Air hissed through his teeth as she stroked her hand down his body, across the tightly held muscles of his abdomen, skimming the hair at its base with her fingertips. Whatever he'd been about to say was gone. Every red blood cell had rushed from his brain as she followed her hand with her mouth, tracing the play of muscles in his belly with her lips and her tongue.

Teasing him for way too long before finally—*finally*—she took his steely length in her hand.

The dark curtain of her hair obstructed his view as it swung and dragged across his taut belly, his flexed thighs and that giant pulsing scream of need in between. She squeezed gently and he jammed his eyes shut. Fisted his fingers in the sheet as her thumb coasted over the head and almost brought him undone. Then she leaned down and breathed, a hot wash of breath against the moisture she'd incited, and the tentative touch of her tongue caused a bolt of sensation that almost lifted him off the mattress.

Her head came up with a start. "Not so good?"

Rafe couldn't stand that flash of uncertainty in her expression, any more than he could stand the torture of her touch.

He slid his hands up the inside of her arms, stretching them over her head, as he rolled her onto her back and followed. Her eyes widened, heat flushed her cheeks as he settled between her legs, as he instantly found the perfect position.

"Too damn good," he growled into her mouth as he kissed her. As she wrapped her legs around his hips and pressed up against him, inviting him into the moist heat of her body. *Too damn good,* he repeated silently, easing his way into that exquisite heat, holding back the urge to go faster. To pull back and just bury himself. Deep. Hard.

That urgency clamored in his blood and tightened in his lungs until he had to end the kiss, to breathe, to press his face into the side of her throat to escape the passionate intensity of her expression.

"That does feel pretty damn good," she whispered and *that* was almost too much. A simple, straight comment that struck him with the same erotic force as the tight clasp of her body closing around him, drawing him deeper, sinking him into her core.

Not just pretty damn good but pretty damn perfect. Pretty damn unforgettable. That's what he wanted for this first time. He wanted to obliterate everything from her sensual memory except him. He wanted momentous where in the past, with every other woman, every other lover, he'd only wanted to satisfy. And for a brief instant of still and silent intensity, their eyes locked and it stunned him how much he wanted...and how much that wanting shook him up.

Sweat beaded on his brow, traced the line of his backbone as he slowly started to move, as he willed himself to set the same torturously slow rhythm he'd used hundreds of times before. He knew how to please a woman, how to drive her wild, how to hit every sweet spot.

How could this time feel infinitely sweeter...more intense...and so damn different?

Because it's only your naked flesh moving in hers, with no barrier and nothing to diminish the pleasure. Because of the expression in her eyes, the soft humming noise in her throat, the grip of her fingers as her hands fluttered under yours.

Because this is Catriona, your wife.

And he couldn't hold back any longer. He released her hands, freed his so he could palm the stretch of her body beneath his, so he could reach between them, between her soft folds to find the supersensitive spot and stroke it with sure pressure.

So he could watch the explosion of heat in her eyes, so he could know that he'd given her the same pleasure that he felt building as he drove harder, deeper, stronger. As he flexed his hips with a last full thrust and let his release come, more powerful than he'd imagined possible, a wild spasm that rocked through his body and reflected in the splintered depths of her eyes as she came again, and he spilled himself deep within her body.

Cat woke slowly. The smile came easily to her lips, the stretch not so easily to her shattered body, and her mind took another ten minutes to get within cooee of cognizance.

Her first random thought was, *Crikey, it's bright!* Eyes squinted against that brightness, she rolled onto her side and checked the bedside clock.

For several ticks, the time displayed made no sense. It couldn't be after ten. She never slept this late, even on holidays.

But she had, and the reason why struck suddenly and with devastating force.

Because of a very late night…a very late *wedding* night.

Her heart thumped loudly in the morning silence. She was alone, she knew, even before she rolled her head on the pillow and inspected the vast stretch of her king-size bed. Even before she lifted up on her elbows and listened to the enveloping quiet that extended beyond her bedroom door.

But she hadn't dreamed up amazing wedding-night sex in her jet-lagged sleep. With her left thumb she touched the gold band on her ring finger. A borrowed wedding band, and that fact chimed, loud and significant, through Cat's sluggish consciousness.

Borrowed because of the whole rushed nature of the event. She barely remembered the moment when he put it on her finger. She barely recalled the vows or where they'd taken them.

How could she be married? How could she have a husband?

How could she have slept so long and so soundly that she didn't even know if he had stayed in her bed or retired to his own? She hadn't heard him leave…but then she didn't recall anything much of afterward. The incredible force of her last climax, the relaxed weight of his body on hers, stroking the cooling sweat over the long planes of his back. Sifting her fingers through his hair and smiling against his throat when he'd murmured something about waking him when she was ready to "just do it" again.

She'd probably fallen asleep with him still there within her arms. Still in her body.

Heat crept through her veins, remembering. Regret stole through her mind, remembering how she hadn't woken him again.

Would he have expected that? Would he have expected

more from her than that once? More times, more variety, more participation? More—

She cut herself off with a sharp mental slap. Rafe Carlisle's critique of her sexual performance didn't matter. Rafe Carlisle as her husband did. She'd married him to regain control of Corroboree, to secure its future in her family. Her hand lifted and paused above her lower abdomen as a whispery flutter of hope stole through her body.

Hope that she could secure that future with a baby…a baby he also needed.

Except they had a lot to work out, to get straight, before any baby came along, and this time Cat would not trust a handshake deal. She'd married Rafe for his money, and he needed to protect his interests as much as she did. With a written contract.

She needed to find him and get this sorted out.

That decision to act sat well with Cat—much better than lying in bed with the morning half-gone. She tossed the bedcovers aside, and—despite the obvious emptiness of the suite—made a quick dash for the closet and the hotel robe inside. The Rafe Carlisles of this world could be as content and arrogant as they liked with their nakedness. The Catriona McConnells needed their robes.

What about the Catriona Carlisles?

That out-of-nowhere thought stopped her short, one hand on the closet door. She sucked in a deep breath—so deep it turned her slightly dizzy. But she gathered herself and shook her head and uttered a grim "No way."

Marrying him didn't include taking his name. She didn't want that kind of link. She didn't want anything beyond what he'd promised in the casino. Not even great, toe-curling, spine-tingling, world-altering sex. She didn't want anything she would miss once he was gone. She wanted—

"Blast."

With a pained grimace she eyed the clothes in the closet—

the ones Bridget had ordered on her behalf after yesterday's shopping extravaganza. She'd forgotten all about returning them; she'd forgotten about everything sensible and practical from the moment he appeared in her doorway.

Well, today was another day, and Bridget could take the clothes back.

Cat slid the robe from its hanger and pulled it on. And when she turned, heading for the bathroom, her eyes snagged on the one dress that wouldn't be going back to the store. The green fabric hung limply from the edge of the chaise, where it must have caught when he tossed it so glibly. A frisson of déjà vu crawled over her skin, a reprisal of that moment in the night when she'd thought about him discarding her.

The morning after, for example.

"Don't be so silly." Impatient with herself, she picked up the dress and flung it into the closet, then jammed the door shut. He'd probably gone to do the business that brought him to Vegas. She didn't expect his attention. She didn't want a big-deal morning after. She was practical, capable, independent Cat McConnell. After her shower, she would find Bridget and arrange to have the clothes returned. The ring, she supposed, would have to go back to the concierge, as well.

Twisting it on her finger, she realized it felt tight. Too tight. She lifted her hand and studied her fingers. They looked a bit swollen. Her feet felt the same, no doubt from the flying and not enough exercise.

Okay, so after her shower, and after she found Bridget, she would go for a long walk. Find a shop that sold cheap and comfortable footwear.

Their flight home from L.A. wasn't until tonight. She had plenty of time, time she would put to good use walking and thinking through what terms to include in their contract.

Rafe had gone downstairs to the jewelers on an impulse. Lying beside her in the bed watching her sleep, fighting the desire to wake her the same way he'd put her into such a sound sleep, he'd caught sight of the ring on her finger. And the beat of desire in his veins changed in nature. Suddenly he'd wanted to wake her with more than a platinum-strength erection. He wanted to surprise her with a ring, her own ring, a symbol of last night's significance.

He hadn't counted on being away long. He hadn't counted on the decision of which stone, which setting, which ring, proving so damn difficult. He'd chosen jewelry for women on countless occasions, but this was different. He wanted it to be special. Unique. A gift she would accept from him without the arguments of yesterday over the clothes.

In the end he couldn't decide, and that sat uneasily on his shoulders as he made the return trip. So did an unfamiliar tension over the gift he *had* bought—a diamond necklace he'd selected because he liked the idea of giving her everything pretty and missing from her hard and frugal life. Because he liked the idea of sliding the cool stones around her neck while she lay naked and sleeping in her bed. Anticipation settled the nervous churn in his belly as he thought about stripping off and slipping into her bed and spending the rest of the day warming them up.

When he opened the door to an empty suite, the swoop of disappointment was intense. But as he walked from room to room looking for a note—a note she apparently hadn't left—his mood shifted from disappointment to discontent. Logic suggested she'd gone for a walk, maybe even looking for him, and that she would be back soon.

He gave her ten minutes.

Then he called the floor concierge and discovered that, yes, she had gone out. But only after searching out Bridget with a request to return the clothes. That rankled. So did her continuing absence past midday, especially when his speculation over her whereabouts turned to Drew Samuels.

Prowling the sitting room, he tossed up whether to call

and ask the cowboy if he'd happened to have seen his wife today. And that turned his mood downright dirty. Not a good time for her to return, but that's when the door opened.

She didn't see him until she'd closed it behind her and crossed the entry foyer. Then she came to an abrupt halt, eyes wide with surprise when they lit on his still figure across the room. If he'd thought the sight of her, home and obviously unharmed, would ease the moody tension in his gut, then he'd been wrong. Dead wrong.

"Bridget said you were looking for me earlier," she said, recovering quickly, "but I thought you'd have gone out again by now."

He could have asked why the hell she'd have thought that, but he was too busy taking in her outfit. *Her* jeans, *her* shirt. A couple of generic plastic bags hung from her hand and slapped softly against her leg as she skirted the dining table into the sitting area.

"You saw Bridget? Was that to check if she'd returned the clothes I bought for you?"

Her eyes narrowed a fraction, probably in response to the frosty tone of his voice. "She saw me by chance, actually. Down in the lobby. Is something the matter?"

Where did he start? Rafe wasn't used to feeling so out of sorts, so close to losing his cool. So rattled by the irrationality of his mood. She was back, right? She'd come to no harm. So, why couldn't he just leave it? Why couldn't he concede that nothing was wrong except his pride over the clothes issue.

And, okay, some justifiable concern over her absence.

"I didn't know where you were," he said tightly. "I've been cooling my heels here, waiting for you to get back."

"I thought you'd be a while dealing with your business."

"My business?"

She paused behind one of the crimson velvet sofas. A wary frown shadowed her eyes as they connected with his. "I assumed that's where you went this morning. To do whatever business brought you here to Vegas."

"I did that last night, Catriona." His gaze dropped to her hand—the *naked* hand—resting on the back of the sofa. He felt every muscle bunch with tension. "Where's your ring?"

"My hands are swollen. I had to take it off."

Rafe couldn't argue with that. He didn't like himself for wanting to argue, for wanting some kind of aggression that was completely foreign and over the top. And he was so caught up in the confusion of his own responses that it took him a long moment to twig to her stillness. To the cooling narrowness of her gaze.

"Was I your business in Vegas, then?" she asked slowly. But she didn't wait for an answer. She gave a slight shake of her head, as if she should have known all along. "All that rubbish about needing to pay me back for getting you out of that plane and taking you in—"

"That wasn't rubbish, Catriona."

"But you brought me here to Vegas meaning to marry me? That was your business?"

"If you put it like that…" Rafe shrugged. "Yes."

"Then don't you think we should have been a little more businesslike? Don't you think we should have ironed a few things out *before* we swapped wedding rings?"

"Things?"

"Terms. Conditions."

"I thought we agreed to our terms last night. I'll pay off your debts. You'll have my baby."

"That's it?" Her voice rose on a note of disbelief. "Don't you think that's a bit sketchy on detail?"

"What do you need to know, Catriona? I'll pay you a monthly allowance, plus wages for a nanny and whatever help you need to run your station."

"Help? What help?"

"A stationhand. Any extra—"

"I don't need a stationhand. I can do my own work. I like it that way!"

"I'm sure you do." Eyes narrowed, Rafe met her mulish expression with unflinching directness. "But what about when you're pregnant? When your belly is way out here, and you can't lift a bale of hay or ride a horse. What about when you're feeding the baby and—"

"Okay, I get your point," she cut in, her voice as tight as hay wire. "But that's a case of *if* I get pregnant. *If* I have a baby."

"That's why I married you."

"In case I'd forgotten?"

Her eyes glittered with more than irritation, more than mulish pride, but in his current mood that's all Rafe wanted to see. "I just wanted to make sure," he drawled, "that we'd got that condition clear."

"Hard not to, given last night."

"Are you complaining?" he asked, deadly soft. "Because I didn't hear you complaining last night. I heard you moaning. I heard—"

"I didn't mean your sexual prowess. I wouldn't be fooling anyone if I complained about that!"

Rafe's gaze narrowed. "Now, why doesn't that sound like a compliment?"

"I'm sure you've heard every compliment I could come up with a hundred times before."

"How do you figure that, Catriona?"

"I figure that because you've likely slept with half the women in Sydney!"

"That many? Just as well I did the blood tests, then!"

Their gazes clashed, blazing with the anger of their exchange and with the knowledge of all they'd shared in the night. "Just as well I'm a sucker," Cat all but hissed after that searing second, "and took your word for it!"

Something glinted hard and sharp in his eyes. Anger? Hurt? Disbelief? Before she could pin it down, he turned and stalked away. He stopped by the piano, the taut lines of his body reflected in the highly polished wood. Then he hit a couple of keys, a delicate tinkling of sound at odds with the stark atmosphere.

At odds with the harsh note of laughter that escaped his throat as he turned back to face her. "Do you really think I'd have lied to you about that?"

Cat shook her head. Expelled a long breath and with it a piece of her white-hot outrage. "I shouldn't have said that. It was uncalled for. I'm sorry if I hurt you."

"You didn't hurt me, Catriona. You disappointed me."

She deserved that. She'd disappointed herself by giving in to the temptation to read up on him on the Internet. And she'd disappointed herself again, just now, by allowing her emotions to derail and overturn a discussion that deserved better.

Inhaling deeply, she concentrated on steadying the churn in her stomach. The uneasy knowledge that she might not be able to get this discussion back on track. But she had to try.

"You mentioned a nanny. For after—*if* I have a baby. Does that mean the baby will live with me?"

"If that's what you want. Yes."

"Of course that's what I want," she said quickly. "But what about you? You're the one who needs the baby. Won't you want to raise your child as a Carlisle? Won't you want to—"

"I'm having this baby because I have to, Catriona, not because I see myself as father material."

"You won't want to be part of his upbringing?" Cat's heart was beating hard. "You don't want custody?"

"While we're married, that won't be an issue."

While they were married—what did he mean by that? Cat moistened her dry mouth. "What kind of marriage are we talking about?"

"The kind where we both keep our independence. That's what you want, right?"

"Yes," she agreed cautiously. "But won't that make it a little hard to have that baby? If I'm living at Corroboree and you're in Sydney?"

"That's the arrangement after we conceive."

Her heart skittered with a panicky sense of foreboding. "And until then…? You can't expect me to live with you in Sydney."

"Why not?"

Why not? *Why not?* "I hate the city. It makes me crazy." Agitated, she lifted her arms, shopping bags and all, then let them drop again. "You didn't mention living in the city when we cut this deal."

"True." Hands in pockets, he leaned negligently against the piano and appeared to consider this. "We need to arrange a compromise."

"What kind of a compromise?"

"You'll stay with me one week a month, act as my wife."

"I don't know how to act as your wife."

Slowly he straightened, eyes glittering with a different kind of heat. "You did fine last night."

"That was sex, Rafe. I don't imagine you want that twenty-four hours a day."

"Don't you?"

Cat's heart danced a tango beat of fear and anticipation as he started to move closer. Blast it. She didn't want to back away. But she didn't trust him, either—him or the heat drifting through her blood and seeping into her skin.

One week a month, in his bed, trying to conceive his baby.

He stopped in front of her, and she forced herself to lift her chin and meet his gaze. To keep this conversation about what mattered. "If I were to stay with you—what else would you expect of me? Do I have to cook? Clean?"

"I have a housekeeper," he said coolly, while his eyes sparked with heat. "I didn't marry you to cook and clean. I married you to be in my bed."

"One week a month, until I conceive. Will that be in the contract?"

"Contract?"

"Yes. I want all the terms and conditions spelled out in a written contract. And there should be something like a pre-nuptial agreement, too."

His eyes narrowed momentarily, then he laughed. Not his usual smooth, silky sound of amusement, not even the earlier harsh sound of disbelief, but a low, edgy sound that snaked through Cat's senses. "What? You don't trust me not to take your station away from you?"

"I mean to protect you. All *your* wealth. When this marriage ends, I don't want anything of yours."

"Anything?" he repeated, dangerously soft.

"Anything other than what we've agreed upon. I don't want anything else from you."

"You've made that abundantly clear, Catriona." Eyes cooler than she'd ever seen them drifted over her, taking in her clothes and lingering on her naked left hand. "Anything else you've failed to drum into me? Anything you think I may have missed?"

No way could she back down from that look of cool disdain. No way could she back away from the challenge in his voice. "There is one thing." She lifted her chin. "I won't sleep with you again until the contract is drawn up and approved."

He stared back at her for a long time while her heart beat hard and high in her throat. A long time while her stomach churned because she could not tell what he was thinking. Too long for her not to point out the deal they'd made on the plane coming to America.

"You promised it would always be my call, Rafe. That you would back off whenever I said so."

"If that's what you want, Catriona." Expression flat, eyes cool, he started to turn away. "I've never imposed myself on any woman. I'm not about to start now."

Ten

A written contract and no sex until it was drawn up, approved and signed.

Not the outcome Rafe wanted for himself or needed for the sake of the will clause. The real bitch of it was how he'd let it get to him for a good two hours after he strolled out of their hotel suite. Yeah, he'd strolled out of there just as coolly as he'd agreed to her terms.

His smarting ego wouldn't let him show how much her lack of trust affected him.

He'd strolled out of the suite and right on down to the hotel casino where he'd done something he hadn't done in close to ten years. He gambled indiscriminately. He lost badly. And he didn't have anyone to blame but his own stupid self.

The money didn't matter. Losing did. He hated the whole concept of loss, and today had to be a landmark day of failure. He'd not only lost at the tables, but he'd lost the exchange of words with Catriona and—worse even than that—he'd lost his cool.

Rafe Carlisle, legend at laidback, king of nonchalant, had got his ego all in a twist because Catriona hadn't played his game his way. Afterward he'd sulked like a kid following a tantrum.

And wasn't that the perfect analogy for his behavior today?

Outside the casino Rafe shook his head in self-disgust. It was his own damn fault for not sorting out the details beforehand. Truth was, he didn't altogether blame Catriona for her stance. She'd been burned in a handshake deal with neighbors she'd known all her life. Friends she'd trusted.

If he'd played his cards right, he would have conceded whatever points she wanted, negotiated a few perks of his own, and parleyed his way right back into her bedroom. Right now she'd be naked except for a cool handful of diamonds around her flushed and sweat-dampened throat.

Rafe patted his jacket pocket where the jewelry box rested. He could go upstairs and present them to her now, along with a bunch of exotic orchids and the world's smoothest apology. But his male pride balked at being set on its bruised backside again today. She could do that, his wife, if he let her. The way she'd done with that crack about other women.

Hell, if he'd slept with a tenth of the women the gossip magazines claimed, there'd be a certain part of him worn-out by now.

No, Rafe wasn't about to present his wife with another chance at putting him down. She wanted a written agreement, and that's what she would get. No pleading, no asking, no cajoling in between.

A contract signed and sealed, and then she would be in his bed. Honoring her side of the deal.

They flew to L.A. late that evening, then met their flight home to Sydney. Over dinner Rafe took the opportunity to talk through Catriona's terms and conditions, making sure they agreed on all the salient points. It was all very cool and civilized, and Rafe hated that fake cordiality almost as much as their earlier confrontation.

Almost.

When they were done eating and conciliating, she politely excused herself, donned headphones and engrossed herself— apparently—in a movie. Rafe swallowed his irritation and muttered, "Don't mind me. I can entertain myself."

But then, watching the nervy flick of her thumbs against middle fingers, he recalled her uneasiness about flying on the trip over and he reached across the dividing console for her hand. She shook her head and mouthed, "No, I'm all right," and he shucked off her rejection with a lazy shrug.

He didn't bother her again.

He made some calls home, checking in with his secretary, booking an early appointment with his lawyer, calling his downstairs neighbor to let her know he'd be back in the morning. Milla had a key so she could look after the cat whenever he was away, and for some reason he didn't like the idea of her bowling in unannounced on Catriona. And since he had the morning meeting with Jack Konrad's law firm, Catriona would be home alone.

It mattered, he discovered with a sharp grab of tension, her first impression of his home. He wanted her to be comfortable. He wanted her to feel as relaxed there as he'd felt at her breakfast table. He wanted her to like it enough that she'd want to extend that one week a month into more.

And he wanted to introduce her into his family. She might not want his fancy clothes or the staff wages he intended to pay on her station, but here was something he could give her free. His family.

That's the call he left until last, but Alex didn't pick up his phone. In the past he'd have gotten a real kick out of irritating his elder sibling with a drawled message on his voice mail. Something like, "Guess what, bro? I got hitched last night in Vegas."

But not today. Not with this news. It was too…hell, he didn't know what. Too serious. Too important. Too—

Frowning, he cut a glance toward the next seat. Found Catriona watching him with a curious intensity. As if she were trying to work something out, too. Something that confused her sleepy hazel eyes, and that unusually soft and vulnerable expression seemed to suck the breath right out of Rafe's lungs.

She blinked slowly and looked away, breaking eye contact and leaving him feeling hollow and, yeah, cheated. Because she hadn't smiled? Because she hadn't maintained her usual direct gaze? Because she'd turned away without a word to explain what was bothering her?

Rafe turned back to his phone with a strange tightness in his chest. A feeling that something had changed right there and then but no one had let him in on the secret. He watched her for another minute, hoping she'd turn back, but she didn't. And suddenly it struck him what had changed.

His attitude.

He wanted more than her, naked and willing, her hands in his hair and eyes linked with his as he came apart deep in her body. He wanted more than great sex, and more than the knowledge that they were each providing the other with something essential.

He wanted more than the essentials. He wanted her respect and her trust. He didn't know how to earn those or even if that was possible, given his reputation and her current attitude. He would try, starting with honoring their handshake deal, keeping his cool, and making her feel comfortable in his home and comfortable with his family.

"I'm on my way home from America," he told Alex's voice mail, after dialing again. "There's someone I'd like you to meet tomorrow. Someone…important. I'll call back in the morning."

Cat completed another aimless circuit of the spacious penthouse, back to where her sole companion watched her with wary circumspection. When she got too close, the Russian blue rose from his perch on a suede window seat and meandered on long, graceful legs to the far end of the living room. A pretty efficient snub, Cat decided, trying not to take it to heart.

"He's shy with strangers," Rafe had explained while he petted the animal's plush silvery coat with long, slow strokes. While fine hairs rose and quivered all over *her* skin. "He'll get used to you."

If I stay long enough.

The words had shimmered through her mind then, and they did again now, three hours later. She wouldn't be able to stand seven days of inactivity. She wouldn't be able to stand feeling this twitchy restiveness, which was almost as bad as the awful awkwardness of the first hour, before Rafe had left for work. Almost as bad as one of the panicky attacks she kept suffering at regular intervals, whenever it struck her that this wasn't all a dream or some Cinderella fantasy.

This was real. This was happening to *her.* She had married this man, and this harborside penthouse apartment was her home, too.

For one week every month.

With a flutter of pulse, her gaze shifted off to the right—to the stairs leading up to the loft-level master bedroom. He hadn't taken her up there during the tour of inspection, but only because she'd demurred. That had been one of the most awful moments of all, when she'd reminded him that she wouldn't be sharing his bed.

"Take whichever bedroom you want," he'd said, apparently unperturbed. "Make yourself at home. I have a meeting to get to but I'll call when I'm finished."

"You don't have to check up on me." Polite, cool, when she was quietly freaking out at being left alone in his too-tidy, too-color-coordinated, too-designer-chic home.. "I'll be fine."

"I'm sure you will be, but I'm waiting on a phone call from my brother Alex. We may be meeting him for lunch."

At the elevator he'd turned and looked back at her in an all-encompassing way that made her heart do a silly skittery thing. A really silly skittery thing given his parting comment.

"You might want to change into a dress for lunch. We'll likely be going to Zarta's."

"Whoever Zarta may be," she'd grumbled at the closing elevator doors. "Like I would know!"

Left with a ton of turbulent energy pumping through her veins and a ton of time on her hands, she'd wanted to get out, to walk, but she was afraid she'd mess up the tricky security system or that she'd walk so far she'd end up lost. And she couldn't ask for directions since she didn't even know his address!

Didn't *that* sum up her situation perfectly? She was married to a stranger, installed in his home, the address unknown.

She took her time showering but she hadn't dressed because she couldn't decide how to dress. Wandering around in a bathrobe, she was still working on whether to defiantly show up in jeans or to compliantly choose from one of the Vegas dresses, which never did get returned to their places of purchase. For the past half an hour of wandering, her sole focus had been that decision. Jeans versus dress. Floral sundress versus pink retro number.

"My God," she told the cat, disgusted with herself. "I am turning into my stepmother!"

Brilliant green eyes stared back at her, unblinking. Not so much as a twitch of his regal Russian tail. Looking at her with the same disdain her stepmother always employed, as if she were not only a blight on the aesthetic landscape but a complete disappointment. The big, raw, homely girl with no fashion sense. Best bury her at the back of the family photo.

Cat thought she'd gotten over caring about that.

"I have," she muttered as she paced another restless circuit of the open-plan living area. It was just this apartment, these surroundings, the decor.

The place had monstrously high ceilings for an apartment and a full wall of glass looking out over Sydney Harbour. She shouldn't feel so confined. Turning, she forced herself to still and look around her. And to acknowledge that her restiveness might not be due solely to the apartment or disturbing thoughts of her stepmother or even the claustrophobic sense of being trapped in a deal that was way out of her league.

Perhaps it was also the notion of meeting his brother.

She hardly even knew her husband. How could she meet his family? How could she smile and shake this brother's hand, knowing that he knew what she knew? That she'd married Rafe out of desperation. For money. And that she'd been chosen, too, for a specific purpose. Looked over and procured for breeding purposes.

An overwhelming gust of anxiety swamped her, leaving her feeling clammy and slightly ill. She hadn't even thought ahead to this scenario or how she would handle it. How she would feel to be introduced to his family.

How they might judge her and find her wanting, the same way her father's new wife had done.

The phone rang, an expensive burr of sound that cut through the quiet but not through her jittery nerves. She couldn't force herself to pick it up. She let it ring out, then she sat on the couch, hugged her knees to her chest and despised herself for being a coward.

Rafe pocketed his phone and cut across some heavy pedestrian traffic toward Phillip Street and the quickest route home. He'd actually hailed a cab before logic intervened with a compelling alternate suggestion. *Take a deep breath, my man, and think again.* In Vegas he'd reacted on raw, unfettered emotion, and look what that coughed up.

A wife he couldn't entice into his bedroom for a look-see, let alone anything hands on.

Thinking about Catriona in his home that morning—restrained, awkward, gaze sliding away from any meaningful eye contact—didn't help his state of mind. Nor did thinking about those hours in Vegas when he'd stewed with worry while she was out taking a walk and buying a few necessities at Walgreens.

She'd likely gone for a walk now. That's why she hadn't answered his call. No reason to rush home for round two of marital mess up.

Turning on his heel, he headed back toward Circular Quay and his office at the harborfront Carlisle Grande. He'd spent the last two hours at Jack Konrad's offices, thrashing out wording and details with a trio of contract experts. Lawyers who'd felt compelled to remind him, at every turn, how much he stood to lose.

Lawyers who hadn't seen the proud set of Catriona's chin when she told him she didn't want anything from him beyond the debt repayment.

In the end he'd had to remind them who was paying whom. And that he wanted the contract drawn today. And until his wife approved and signed that document, he figured it best he keep away from any one-on-one encounters, especially at his apartment where his irritation over the bedroom arrangement would not stand another round of testing.

If, in fact, she was still at his apartment.

Worry shadowed his footsteps but he kept on walking.

When he got back to his office, he would call again….

"Catriona?"

"Yes. I'm here."

Breathy, and with the briefest hesitation, but at least she'd answered this time. Rafe shifted from his tense perch on the edge of his desk, slumping into his chair and closing his eyes for a second. A ridiculous intensity of relief wiped his mind clear of everything except instinct, and he said what he'd wanted to say early that morning, when he'd taken her into his home for the first time. "I'm glad you're there."

She was silent for a beat, and then her voice—still husky, still hesitant—came through the line again. "Sorry I didn't answer before. I was…in the bathroom."

"I thought you must have gone out."

"Out…where?"

"For a walk." *Or a drive to, say, the airport.*

"I thought about it."

"But?"

"I wasn't sure about getting back in," she admitted in a rush. "I know you told me about the security, but my mind was so thick from flying and I…I didn't want to end up locked out."

Rafe swore silently. He'd been so busy keeping his instinctive responses in check, so busy thinking ahead to the contract that would set them straight again—that would get her moved upstairs and into his bed tonight—that he'd neglected the basic essentials. Like introducing her to the doorman and ensuring she knew her way around. Making sure she had money. "I'm sorry. I should have—"

"It's not your fault. This morning was…"

Her voice trailed off and Rafe chuckled. He found that lack of description oddly descriptive. "Yeah. It was."

"I didn't want things to be like that between us, because of what I said in Vegas," she said softly. "I'm sorry."

"Me, too." And thinking about all the things he was sorry about chased the earlier amusement from his voice. "I will make it up to you, baby."

Silence followed, a quiet flavored with his fervent hope that she was on the same wavelength when it came to making it up.

"The contract should be ready this afternoon," he told her.

"That quick? Will I get to see a draft?"

"If you want."

"Of course I want," she retorted.

Now that sounded more like the old Catriona! With a soft grunt of satisfaction, Rafe kicked back in his chair. "We can do that after lunch. Give them time to make amendments—" *while I take you shopping for a ring* "—so we can sign before the end of business."

"After lunch…with your brother?"

"Yeah. Do you like seafood?"

A two-note laugh bubbled from the phone.

"Is that a no?"

"No. That was just my nervous commentary on how little we know about each other!"

Not the response he'd expected, but… "Here's your chance to fill in another blank…seafood or Japanese? Or would you rather—"

"I'd rather not go at all."

Rafe frowned. "Is this about meeting Alex? He isn't as scary as he looks, you know. There's even the occasional strange woman who finds him charming."

"It's too soon to be meeting family," she said in a rush. "I need to get used to the notion myself first."

"So this is a postponement?"

Silence.

"I want to introduce you to my family." And he hadn't anticipated her resistance. Nor had he anticipated the primitive cut of emotion that snapped on its heels. "I want to introduce you as my wife. As Catriona Carlisle."

Her sharp intake of breath hissed through the receiver. "Catriona *McConnell* Carlisle."

"If you like." Rafe didn't care what she put in the middle, but he did care about the spark in her comeback. That was the Catriona he knew, not the stiff, polite stranger of this morning. Now all he had to do was figure out a way to get that spirited woman to the restaurant. "So, what have you been doing all morning?"

"Nothing."

"I bet you don't get to kick back nearly enough. Feet up, eyes closed, nothing to do but pass the time—"

"I'm not coming to lunch," she said, obviously seeing right through his ploy. "No matter how bored I am."

"What are you going to do, then?"

"I need to get out, take a walk."

Rafe sighed. Okay, so she wasn't about to relent on the lunch date, but he could at least make sure she found her way back inside after her walk. That she was there when he dropped by after lunch to take her into the city. Those plans he wasn't changing. "I'll get Milla to come up and walk you through the security thing again."

"Who's Milla?"

"Just a friend who lives downstairs. She looks after Tolstoy when I'm away."

For some reason her lack of response felt meaningful, although for the life of him Rafe couldn't figure out why.

"Catriona?"

"This…Milla. She isn't the lady who owned your cat. You know, originally?"

"Hell, no." He laughed softly, tickled with that notion. And with the motivation behind her question. His voice dropped a semitone to ask the question he couldn't resist. "Jealous?"

"Should I be?"

"No, but I like that you are." Yeah, he liked that spark of possessiveness a lot. But he also remembered in Vegas when she'd cut into him about the women in his past. He didn't want her sitting there, alone in his apartment, getting crazy thoughts. "I'll ask Milla to come up," he told her. "And, Catriona…"

"Yes?"

"You know there are women in my past—not as many as you'd like to believe, but enough. They're in my past. They stay in my past. There's only one thing to remember." He paused a beat. "I chose you, Catriona Carlisle. Only you."

* * *

A part of Cat wanted to believe his deep note of sincerity, and for a while after she hung up the phone, she indulged that fanciful place by stretching out on the plush sofa and enjoying the little thrills of he-picked-me delight. She wanted to believe in the fairy tale where the wildly handsome prince chose the plain but plucky heroine as his soul mate and rescued her from her loneliness.

Then the neighbor came visiting and knocked that silly little fantasy right back where it belonged.

Rafe had described Milla as "just a friend who lives downstairs." Cat didn't think she could be described as "just" anything. Not "just" svelte, not "just" stylish, not "just" as darkly exotic as her name. She was stop-and-stare stunning.

Especially when she smiled with what appeared to be genuine warmth as she introduced herself. "Rafe said you needed some company, but please let me know if I'm intruding. He tells me to get lost quite regularly. I expect you to do the same when warranted!"

Cat doubted that any male would ever tell a woman who looked like Milla to get lost. Tolstoy illustrated that point by—after taking a wide and exaggerated path around her to get to their visitor—winding his lithe body around her legs and mewing to be picked up.

With a soft peal of laughter and a few crooned words of greeting, she complied. Tolstoy purred in her arms. Any male would do the same, Cat figured.

And she realized that her silence had stretched too long. "Sorry," she said quickly. "You caught me unawares a bit. I'm Catriona McConnell."

"Hmm. A little bird told me you were Catriona *Carlisle*." Milla wrinkled her perfect nose disarmingly. "It takes a bit of getting used to the change, doesn't it?"

"You're married?"

"I was. Twice, actually. Probably best you don't ask. I'd hate to color your newlywed bliss with my cockeyed cynicism."

Cat didn't know quite how to respond. In the space of a minute her emotions had rocketed all over the universe. From her pleasurable little fantasy after Rafe's phone call to stunned awe at Milla's appearance. From depressed how-can-I-compete to aren't-I-a-goose, she-isn't-competition relief.

Now curiosity licked through her blood, lighting dangerous need-to-know spot fires. About Milla's twice-married state, but mostly about her relationship with Rafe.

"Would you like coffee?" she asked. "Or something to drink?"

"We can do that or would you rather go out somewhere? I don't mind waiting while you get ready."

Cat wondered how long she was prepared to wait, given that her hair was an unbrushed mess from her shower and she didn't have a clue what to wear. Milla wore casual, but her jeans were white and designer smart. Her T-shirt a statement in less is more. Her straight, midnight-dark hair was clipped into one of those artless messes of a ponytail that only suit the sleek and beautiful. On Cat, that style would have attracted nesting birds.

Feeling decidedly overwhelmed and underprepared, she took the easy route. "I'd as soon stay in, if that's all right with you."

"Settled." And with easy confidence Milla headed for the kitchen. "I'm a tea drinker myself—what about you?"

Cat followed slowly. Stood at the edge of the terrazzo tiles watching the downstairs neighbor put her hands on everything she needed as if she'd done the same a hundred times before. All the while Milla chatted—effortlessly—about varieties of tea and the merits of drinking from fine bone china. Elegant and expensive, she fit the decor as smoothly as the black marble countertops and sleek silvery backsplashes.

She fit the apartment and Rafe's lifestyle in a way that Cat never would, no matter how many shopping expeditions or spa visits he treated her to. Her heart did a heavy-handed stop-start maneuver high in her chest as she recalled his words on the phone earlier, his comment about the women in his past and how he had chosen her.

Could she believe him? Did she trust his word? Would she ever fit into his life?

Or was she setting herself up for another failure, a second heartbreak at the hands of a smooth-talking charmer?

Eleven

With Milla leading the way, they took their tea upstairs to a rooftop terrace beyond the master bedroom. Since she hadn't allowed Rafe to take her up those stairs, she didn't know about the terrace…not that she was about to let on. She was, after all, supposed to be enjoying newly wedded bliss. And she should have experienced some of that newly wedded bliss in the big, bold bed that dominated his sparsely furnished bedroom.

As they passed, Cat couldn't help taking a peek. The bed sat on a platform one step up, so that at first glance it appeared to float above the ebony floor. Heat trickled through her senses as she imagined Rafe lazing back on the heaped cushions, his mouth curved in a come-hither smile….

"Great bed, isn't it?"

Like a bucket of cold water, Milla's voice washed down on that warm sensual image. Milla, whose relaxed attitude in this apartment was raising little prickles of alarm along Cat's nerve endings. The kitchen was one thing. Hopping uninvited to the master bedroom level with "great bed" comments something else again.

Feeling vastly out of sorts with the whole setup—and with herself for allowing her visitor to take charge—she took a seat and pulled the tea tray to her side of the table so she could pour.

Unperturbed, Milla waved an elegant arm at the vista. "What do you think? It's bloody stunning, isn't it?"

Cat's sound of agreement was probably colored with her testy mood because her companion slanted her a long, measured look. "Too much?"

"Higher rent than I'm used to."

Milla asked about where she was used to; Cat told her about Corroboree. A nice, polite, innocuous conversation over tea that lapsed into silence, neither awkward nor comfortable. Cat decided that—on her side at least—it was wary.

"I imagine you'll be going to the Wentworth show on Friday night," Milla said eventually.

She would? To hide her cluelessness Cat took a long sip of her tea. Made a noncommittal sound.

"If you need a hairdresser—" Cat felt the other woman's gaze drift over her tangled curls "—I can recommend my gal. And since she's coming here to do me, she might be able to fit you in, as well."

If she were going to any Friday-night "show"—this had to mean a society party of some kind—Cat would need help. Big help. But sharing that help with this woman... "Thank you for the offer." She put down her cup. "But I'll manage."

"Sure?"

"I haven't even decided if I'm going." Hardly a lie, since she didn't yet know what Rafe expected of her, socially. "I'm not so big on parties."

"You know, I don't blame you. Those things can be brutal at the best of times and you will be the center of attention."

"Because I'm with Rafe?"

Milla laughed. "Because you're *married* to Rafe, sweetie. Everyone is going to want to size up the lucky duck who snagged bachelor number one!"

Despite the balmy spring temperature, Cat felt herself go cold. Why hadn't she thought of that? She'd read the articles, damn it, on the Internet. All that interest in the Carlisle brothers' private lives. All those insinuations she'd sniped at him about in Vegas. She'd been so busy worrying about meeting his family that she hadn't spared a thought for the larger population.

The laughter faded from the other woman's face. She leaned forward a little, her voice gentle. "Hey, I was joking, you know."

"Were you?"

Milla grimaced. "Not about the interest in you, unfortunately. But about snagging Rafe, yes. We both know that happened the other way around!"

That Rafe had snagged her? True, she supposed, in a way. But now she wondered how much Milla knew. How much her husband had shared with this just-a-neighbor he'd sent to keep her company. "Rafe told you how we met?"

"You rescued him from a crashed plane, I believe. How romantic!"

No, it hadn't been romantic. It had been practical. But Cat bit her tongue from making that distinction out loud.

"I'm glad he found you." A surprising sincerity steadied the other woman's exotically dark eyes as she held Cat's gaze across the table. "Rafe is a much better man than he lets on, even to himself. He deserves someone gutsy and real. He deserves better than a bimbo like Nikki!"

Cat's heart began to soar like the gulls over the harbor before them, then dipped and dove on the last word. She had to ask. She couldn't not. "Who is Nikki?"

Slowly Milla put down her cup. Her expression looked pained, caught out, and she took a long time to answer. As if she were choosing her words with deliberate care. "He was flying out to see her...when he met you."

Understanding cannoned through Cat, tightening her chest and her throat. A constriction that squeezed every last remaining drop of her earlier fantasy from her consciousness. "He was flying to see her...to ask her...when the storm put him down? At my place?"

The answer was obvious. Milla didn't have to say a word, although she made a rueful moue. "Rafe has always had the most sensational luck!"

Yes, Cat couldn't help thinking. How lucky to have landed on the doorstep of a sucker. A sucker who hadn't even seen it coming. Even when he'd lazed against her kennel enclosure and joked about paying someone to have his baby. Even when he'd stood in the middle of a Las Vegas casino and offered her one "win-win" spin of the wheel.

Even when he'd said, *I chose you, Catriona. Only you.*

It was another of his lines, another of his sweet-talking, get-his-own-way lines. And she, prize sap number one, had fallen for it body and soul.

Milla left, but her impact remained, as subtle as the lingering scent of her perfume, as pervasive as the hurt centered in Cat's chest. It wasn't her heart, though. It was her pride that hurt, because she'd wanted to believe in those momentary senses of connection. She'd wanted him to have chosen her for something more personal than convenience. She'd wanted it to have been *only you.*

But no, he'd intended to ask someone named Nikki. Then, because of circumstances, luck, fate, the vagaries of weather, he'd landed at her place and transferred his goal onto her. She tried to remember that morning in the guest room, the kitchen, the kennels. Tried to recall if he'd said where he was going before the storm hit. Perhaps she hadn't ever asked.

"Can you believe that?" she murmured, but nobody heard.

Tolstoy had skulked out of the living area after Milla's departure, and that desertion felt like another crushing blow to her pride. Silly, since the cat's only previous communication was via a disdainful stare.

Silly, too, that she should feel this alone in the center of Australia's biggest city.

At Corroboree she'd spent years on her own but she'd never felt this thick choking sense of abandonment. At home her *alone* was filled with the morning call of birds, the background chatter of open radio, the bellow of cows calling to their calves. The creak of old boards shifting with the change of temperature. The sound of the lilac tree scraping against her bedroom window, or Sheba yapping at a possum as it scampered from rooftop to orchard.

Suddenly Cat felt an intense yearning for the familiarity of the outback where she belonged. Sitting on his plush sofa, she closed her eyes and tried to force it aside, to remember that Rafe would be back in an hour or two to take her to check the contract.

The contract that would bind them together, that would make this marriage more real than their Vegas vows.

Her need to escape, to go home to the place where she was herself—the strong and capable Catriona McConnell, a woman she liked—came back at her again in a great big wave that rocked her with its force. She didn't belong here in this expensive world filled with beautiful people and Friday-night "shows" that required hairdressers and promised to put *her* in the spotlight.

Not Catriona McConnell, not even Catriona Carlisle, but Mrs. Rafe Carlisle.

Her mind and her stomach churned. This wasn't real life— not *her* real life. She should never have agreed to live here for a week. She should never have agreed to this marriage as a quick fix for her financial problems or to fill the void of her missing family.

Marrying him was a dumb rebound thing that could only end in heartbreak. A couple of days in his company, one night with him in her bed, and she'd tumbled halfway into love. Or lust. Or something somewhere in between the two.

She shot up from the sofa and started to pace.

Surely they could annul this sham of a marriage. People did that spur-of-the-moment Vegas thing all the time and got out of it.

And what about your debt? What about Corroboree?

Slowly she sank back down onto the sofa and clutched her head in her hands. She couldn't think straight here. She had to get away—except how? She didn't have enough money in her bank account to pay a bus fare, let alone a plane ticket.

Fraught with anxiety she scanned the possibilities and came up with only one.

Was she that desperate?

Did she need to escape to her home that urgently?

Sick with the decision she needed to make, her stomach pitched. But she sucked in a breath and reached for the phone. Waited an agonizing beat of five seconds before her stepmother answered. Before she sucked up her pride and asked her to buy the ticket that would take her home.

"What the hell happened, Catriona?"

When she finally answered her phone, it was after nine that night and Rafe didn't bother with preliminaries or small talk. He'd spent close to seven hours trying to read between the lines in the short message she'd left on his voice mail.

"I'm sorry, Rafe, but I have to go home. I have responsibilities there and I should never have agreed to stay with you in Sydney. I need to think this whole thing through before we go any further. I can't think here. I need to be home."

She—as he'd noted before they went to Vegas—had no facility for leaving messages, so by the time she finally did pick up he was struggling against a wall of simmering emotions. He struggled, too, to contain his impatience while he waited for her response to that straight-to-the-point opening.

"Did you get my message?" she hedged.

"Couldn't you have waited another hour and told me in person?"

"There's only one afternoon flight. I had to leave to make the airport in time."

"Milla said you never mentioned a word to her about leaving. Half an hour later, you're gone. Why?" He paused, slammed a hand through his hair, forced himself to stop pacing. "Is there something wrong at Corroboree? Did you get a phone call?"

"No. I…" She paused and he heard her draw a breath. "This isn't going to work."

"This?"

"Us. This relationship. You should have stuck with Nikki."

Rafe went very still. "Nikki?"

"Your first choice. Her name's Nikki, isn't it? You were flying out to see her, to ask her to have your baby, the day the storm forced you down."

"Who told you that?"

"Does it matter?"

No, it didn't. She was right. What mattered was the fact that she was five hundred miles away. That for some reason—maybe it was Nikki, maybe it was more—she'd decided to run away from their deal. "We have an agreement, Catriona. The night you married me in Vegas I told you to be very sure. I said there would be no going back."

"You also said you chose me. Only me."

"I didn't mislead you, Catriona. I decided on you the day after we met. Nothing has happened since to change my mind and I can't think of anything I've done that should have changed yours."

"It's not any one thing—"

"Good," he cut in, not giving her a chance. This wasn't something he would debate over the telephone. "Because the contract is drawn and ready for signing. I promised you a draft, and *I* honor my promises. I'll e-mail the document tonight."

"I won't sign anything until I'm sure I'm doing the right thing."

"If you want to keep Corroboree, you don't have a choice. My lawyer has spoken to Samuels. That part of our deal is already in motion. All you have to do is sign the agreement, Catriona. You have forty-eight hours to request any changes. Otherwise, I'll see you Friday morning."

"You're coming down here?" Her voice rose on a note of anxiety, and Rafe smiled with a perverse sense of satisfaction. She had cause to worry. If he had to chase halfway across the country to make her uphold her end of the deal, then he intended making the trip very worthwhile.

"I'll see you Friday, Mrs. Carlisle," he said, and hung up.

Cat returned the amended draft of their contract because she didn't have any choice. It was up to him now, whether he accepted her changes or not. She didn't expect he would. She did expect another heated phone call, and spent many agitated hours pacing around her office on Wednesday and Thursday nights, waiting for the instrument to ring.

It didn't, and his silence caused her even more misgivings.

She did receive two e-mails. The first reported that he'd installed a message bank on her phone service. The second was a scanned invitation for the Friday-night event Milla had mentioned. The "Wentworth show," apparently, was a fashion fund-raiser for a children's hospital, and the Carlisle Hotel Group was a major sponsor.

Cat stared at the invitation with intense trepidation—she would rather wrestle a pit full of tiger snakes than a room full of fashionistas all eager to size her up—but that quickly morphed into consternation. What did this mean? He'd said he was coming here on Friday—had he changed his mind? He hadn't included any note of explanation. Did he expect her to hurry back to Sydney on the strength of this invitation?

No way. And no way would she give him the satisfaction of calling to find out. Maybe that was stupid and stubborn of her, but she wanted to imagine she could hang on to her pride since he'd taken a grip on too much of her life.

Coming home had not been all she'd imagined while sitting on his plush sofa back in Sydney: she hadn't slept worth a bean; she'd gained little comfort from the hollow emptiness of her home. Only her dogs made it worthwhile with their enthusiastic adoration.

By Friday morning she was completely frazzled and out of sorts. But she got on with her work and she worried about whether he would turn up as she watched the sky for any sign of his plane.

"Not that I know what kind of plane to watch out for," she told Bach. Her worried eyes scanned the eastern horizon yet again.

I should have called. I should have told him to use Gordon's strip. I don't want to hear an engine overhead and go through another rough landing...or worse.

What would her pride be worth then?

"I'll call," she decided. "As soon as we get these cattle yarded, I will call."

With a new sense of urgency she gunned her trail bike around the heifers she was bringing in for drenching. Bach skirted the flanks of the mob, hurrying the stragglers.

They were within a stone's throw of the yards when she saw the plume of dust on her driveway. Her heart skittered.

"Silly," she muttered, although her gaze remained glued on that approaching speck of a vehicle. Her heart continued to skip and skate. "He wouldn't drive."

Even from the airport?

Even from another strip?

A recalcitrant heifer attempted to break, and she forced herself to concentrate on her job, keeping the mob intact as she herded them toward the holding yard. When she looked back toward the road again the vehicle had disappeared. Her lungs felt constricted, tight with anticipation as she waited for its reappearance from behind the homestead.

Ridiculous, but she knew in her bones that it was him. Knew before the white Landcruiser came back into view, heading now for the yards. The air wheezed in her lungs as she sucked in a deep breath and attempted to steady the frantic beat of her heart.

Gordon Samuels's vehicle. Just one figure in the cabin. The silhouette too tall, too refined, too familiar to that wildly beating heart to be anyone but Rafe.

She kicked down the stand on her bike and swung her leg over the seat. *Walk to the yards, Catriona. Shut the gate, secure the chain. Don't forget to breathe.* Simple everyday things she was having trouble remembering.

And when she turned around he was getting out of the vehicle. Long legs in dark trousers. Dark shirt. Dark designer shades. A shiver of heat chased through her veins as his head came up and his shaded gaze fixed on her. He'd never looked more out of place, standing there in the red dust kicked up by a hundred milling cattle, and before Cat could start crossing that space between them she had to remind herself to breathe again.

A dozen emotions pounded Rafe as he watched her approach, all of them expected, most of them tight and tumultuous, none of them evident on his face. He kept his expression schooled, the same as his posture and the lazy cadence of his voice as he asked, "What the hell do you think you're doing?"

A spark of irritation lit her eyes as she lifted her chin and met his gaze from under the broad brim of her stockman's hat. "I'm working. As some of us do. Is that a problem?"

"I told you I was coming today."

"And here you are. Should I have been waiting at the homestead?"

Rafe ignored the sweet sarcasm in that question and allowed a smile to curve his mouth. "That would have made things easier. But that's never on your priority list, is it?"

The sting registered in her eyes, in the tightening of her lips. Good. She needed to know he'd had enough of her contrary behavior and stalling tactics.

"This—" he lifted his chin to indicate the cattle at her back "—looks like a job in progress."

"I'm about to start drenching."

"I assume this won't take long?"

Her gaze narrowed. "Why would you assume that?"

"Because we have business to conclude." Straightening, Rafe tapped a hand against the roof of the Landcruiser. "I gather you recognize this vehicle?"

The dog crouched at her feet growled. Her voice held a similar edge when she said, "Of course I do. I assume you wisely chose to use his airstrip."

"That was convenient. Seeing as I also hand delivered a cheque."

A flinch of emotion crossed her face but her gaze remained fixed and narrow on his. "You paid off my debt with Samuels? But I haven't signed the contract."

"Are you going to?"

"Did you make the alterations?"

"Would you sign if I hadn't?"

She didn't answer. She didn't need to.

Rafe smiled. "I figured as much. That's why I let you have your changes."

"All of them?"

"I expected you'd want to halve every payment or allowance I wanted to give you. That's why I doubled them in the first place."

Shock widened her eyes and widened Rafe's satisfaction as he watched her take that aboard. "What about the clause I crossed out?" she asked, recovering. "The one about spending a week a month in Sydney?"

"I hated approving that one, but I did."

"Why?" Obviously nonplussed she spread her arms, palms up. "Why would you do that? And why would you pay off Samuels without my signature?"

"I was always going to do that, Catriona."

She stared back at him, still and quiet, for a long moment. "And what if I don't sign now?"

"That's your prerogative."

"What if I've decided that this whole marriage is a complete sham and I can't do it anymore? I mean, that's possible isn't it? People annul those quickie Vegas marriages all the time. No one need even know."

"Don't you think it's a little late for that?"

Knowledge flared in her eyes. Knowledge of wedding-night heat, of all they'd shared, of what they may have created.

"Even if you're not pregnant, Catriona—" he let his gaze drift down to where one of her hands hovered near her belly, and he felt a deep and rich stirring in his "—there are others who know we got married."

"Your brother. And your neighbor."

"*Your* neighbor, too."

"You told Samuels? Did you have to?"

Renewed irritation burned in Rafe's belly at her indignant tone. "Why is that such a problem? Would you prefer he spread the word that you'd slept with me in return for that cheque?"

"Isn't that what I did?"

"No, Catriona. You married me." And this time he didn't attempt to hide his irritation or his impatience. "I have a contract in the vehicle that you asked for, with amendments you requested. Sign it or not, that's your choice. What matters to me is the deal we made in Vegas, the vows we exchanged in that chapel and in your bed."

A pulse fluttered in her throat, heat rose in her cheeks. But her voice, when she finally spoke, was clear and even. "And after I sign?"

"I would like you to come back to Sydney with me. For the weekend."

"Because of this charity thing tonight?"

"Yes."

She moistened her lips. "You wouldn't want to take me to something like that. I'd hate it."

"How do you know that?"

"I know, okay?"

But beyond the obstinate answer he saw a glimmer of appeal in her eyes that he couldn't refuse. And, hell, if he could just get her to sign the contract after that panicky talk about annulment he'd be happy.

And afterward…well, afterward he intended to make them both very happy.

"So—" he looked beyond her at the cattle "—how long should it take us to knock this lot over?"

"Us?"

Rafe's gaze rolled back to lock on hers. "I'm going to help you, Catriona. And in return you're going to tell me the whole story about what happened on Tuesday to send you running home."

Cat didn't bother objecting to his help—she could see he meant business—and that help more than halved the time taken. There was no opportunity to talk about her flight from his apartment. With one of them feeding the draft and the other on the drenching gun, they weren't ever working side by side, so their conversation was restricted to shouted instructions and the odd passing remark about the job they were doing.

They returned to the homestead separately and met up

again over a cold drink of water in her kitchen. She thanked him for his help, and he grinned and thanked her for letting him help. "I haven't done any cattle work in years. I enjoyed myself."

"Really?"

He told her how all three brothers learned the ropes at an early age on Kameruka Downs, going out on stock camps during their July and October school holidays.

"I never pictured you as a cowboy," she said.

"There's a lot you don't know about me," he countered.

A frisson of unease skittered through her bones, not because of all she didn't know about him but because of all she did. She suspected the negligent playboy charmer thing was just a clever disguise. When it came down to it, he could do purposeful as well as anyone she'd ever met. And he had such a way of twisting things around to get what he'd wanted all along.

Is this what he'd wanted?

The two of them together in her house, her day's work finished with an afternoon stretching long and lazy before them?

She looked up and found him watching her in a way that chased all thought from her mind and all breath from her lungs. It was the look of a hunter eyeing its prey. A look of intensity and purpose and soul-searing heat.

Cat's heart thundered. She put down her glass, carefully, afraid it might slip through her trembling fingers. Despite the water she'd just finished, her mouth felt thick and dry. "I'd like to take a look at that contract now."

"If you like." He lifted a shoulder, casual, negligent, while his eyes told another story entirely. "I'd like to take a shower…if that's all right."

"Of course. I'll just make sure there's a towel."

Inside the guest bathroom, she slumped against the wall a moment to catch her breath and think. Except, all she could think about was the last time Rafe had used this bathroom…and that he'd soon be naked here again. All she could picture was the look in his eyes across her kitchen, and when she opened her eyes he was there, in the door of the bathroom.

Not yet naked but working on it.

Twelve

"**W**hat do you think you're doing?"

The squeaky rise in her voice and the flush of heat in her cheeks gave Rafe no end of satisfaction. He'd followed her into the bathroom to catch her off guard while she found him a towel, and while her guard was down he intended finding out what had gone wrong in Sydney. Here they wouldn't be working at opposite ends of a cattle draft. Here she would be naked and unable to escape.

He dropped his shirt on the bathroom floor and met the nervous flicker of her eyes as they rose from his bare chest to his face. "I told you I was taking a shower," he said.

"And I said I was making sure you had a—"

Rafe peeled off trousers and underwear in one efficient pass and straightened. "A…towel?"

Her gaze whipped back up to his. "You could have waited until I'd finished in here."

"I could have. But then I remembered how you liked efficiency." Eyes still linked with hers, he reached into the shower enclosure and turned on the taps. "I thought we'd save time by getting two things out of the way at once."

"Two things?"

Her voice was barely audible above the hiss of the shower as he leaned into the water to test the temperature. When he straightened and raked his dripping hair back from his face, she licked a nervous tongue across her lips. Anticipation surged in his body, a solid rush of heat beneath the cool patina of wet skin.

"Two things...or possibly three." Slowly he closed the space between them, smiling as he backed her up against the vanity. "If you ask nicely."

Her eyes flashed, cross, indignant, but the effect was spoiled by her quick intake of breath when he rested his hands on the vanity on either side of her hips. Trapping her inches from the jut of his aroused body.

"What are the first two?" she asked.

"Getting clean." His gaze swept over her dusty face and braided hair. "And having that conversation I mentioned earlier."

Her mouth opened but all that came out was a wheezy gasp as he straightened, wrapped his arms around her and started backing toward the shower. "What are you doing?"

"Let's start with getting clean."

Her eyes widened with shock as he walked them both under the water. He hadn't planned this part, but it seemed to be working out well. He'd definitely caught her off guard. Her hands flapped uselessly, trapped at her side. "My clothes," she spluttered. "They're getting soaked."

"We'd best get them off you, then."

But before he let her down, Rafe turned them a half circle until she was cornered in the small enclosure. Barricading her there with his body, he started unbuttoning her shirt. Of course she protested. Naturally she batted at him with her hands, but he used his elbows to block her arms, and when she tried to duck out of reach he took advantage of her widened stance to press a naked thigh between her jeans-clad ones.

She sucked in a shuddery breath, but her wide eyes snarled in a satisfying way. "You said you'd never imposed yourself on a woman."

"I'm not imposing."

"You're just taking?"

That gave him pause.

His gaze rose swiftly to meet hers, but Cat found it hard to focus on their sea-green complexity. The heels of his hands rested on her breasts, distracting her with their rough-edged heat even through the soaked fabric of her shirt. She attempted to focus instead on the tiny pulse that beat at the corner of his jaw.

"I think you have the wrong idea, wife." Very deliberate, very slow, he leaned closer and she felt the increased pressure of every point of contact. Shock waves of heat pulsed through her breasts and tightened in her nipples. She didn't realize his purpose until he'd rolled back, the bottle of shower wash in his hand. "I'm only washing you. And your clothes, too. Efficient, aren't I?"

He pumped a glob of the creamy wash into the palm of each hand, then smoothed it over her chest, tracing her collarbone and the swell of her breasts above her bra. Then while she was still savoring that delicious touch of sensory pleasure, he efficiently peeled off her shirt and slung it over the glass partition.

"Turn around."

Cat obeyed. She felt his hands at her back, unhooking her bra, sliding the straps down her arms until it, too, was gone.

"Can you hold your plait up, out of the way?"

She did, and he made a soft sound of approval in his throat. A perfect accompaniment to his hands as they slicked the body wash over her shoulders and back.

"We worked well together today, don't you think?"

He expected her to think? With his big hands making those slow, gliding strokes over her back and down her sides. Teasing the outsides of her breasts with each pass. Closer and closer. Slower and slower. With a low groan she slumped forward and pressed her forehead against the cool tiles.

"We work well together in other ways, too."

His voice was close to her ear, a low rumble of heat in her blood as his hands slid around her ribs. As his thumbs stroked the underside of her breasts.

Then retreated.

The breath left her lungs in a hot gust of frustration. But when she tried to turn around he pressed a splayed a hand across her abdomen and held her there. Trapped between the wide spread of those fingers and the wall of hard, wet body at her back. Trapped in a web of wanting that twined through her, as warm and slow and liquid as the gentle wash of water on their bodies. As warm and slow and liquid as his open-mouthed kiss against the side of her throat.

"I'm not taking," he murmured, moving that sensuous mouth up to nip at her earlobe. "I'm giving."

And, finally, his hands closed over her breasts, cupping each with finely textured skin and finely hewn restraint. Cat didn't give a damn who was giving or taking or receiving. Shamelessly turned on, she arched her back and drew a long breathy moan of pleasure at the dual friction of her nipples against his palms and her backside against his erection.

"Can I take off my jeans?" she asked.

"Not yet."

His hands slid from her breasts, down over her abdomen to rest at her hipbones.

She turned her head, frowned at this lessening of contact. "You said you were washing me."

"And your clothes."

"Well, you're taking your time and that isn't efficient!"

He laughed, low and gruff and sexy. "If I take off your jeans, I'm likely to get very inefficient. And I haven't washed your hair, yet."

Cat growled impatiently as he rolled away from her back, but then his hands were in her hair, unbraiding her plait, separating the thick sections and playing them against her skin. Working a thick lather of shampoo, massaging her scalp, turning her weak with the impact of that whole sensual experience.

The brush of wet skin, belly to back, as he leaned past her to reshelve the bottle. His hands smoothing a delicious path from her shoulders down her arms until they closed over her hands and linked their fingers. His face nuzzling her wet hair aside, his mouth at the junction of her shoulder, kissing, biting, sucking.

The press of his body at her back and the sweet ache of hunger in her blood and her body.

"My hair is done," she said, and her voice felt as thick as her blood, as clumsy as the fingers that struggled to unsnap her jeans. "Can you get this blasted thing?"

His laughter rasped over her as he turned her around. As he stroked those wonderful hands over her shoulders and upper arms and kissed her and kissed her and kissed her. Most inefficient, she thought, but then his hands were at her waist and tugging at her jeans and she decided he might just be getting the message.

He released her mouth with a last long stroke of heat, tongue to tongue, a last nip of her bottom lip, and his half-lidded gaze lifted to hers. "We are having that conversation."

Talk? Coherently? Was he serious?

"I want to start by making one thing clear." He lifted his hands and cupped her face, a gentle, cool contrast to the searing intensity of his eyes. "I haven't thought about another woman since I opened my eyes in that Cessna."

Cat blinked. "Why are you telling me this now?"

"In case you need any reassurance."

"I need," she said slowly, "you to take off my jeans."

One corner of his mouth lifted but his hands didn't move from her face. "I'll get to that. After you tell me why you ran away."

"That's blackmail."

"Let's just call it enticement."

He leaned forward and kissed her again. And because of the sweet hunger in that kiss and the straight heat of his gaze and, yes, the enticement of getting his clever hands to soap where her jeans now covered, she met his eyes with complete honesty. "I was homesick. And scared. I panicked."

"Scared of…?"

"Your home…it's so…" How could she explain? How could he expect her to find words with him naked and—

"You don't like my home?"

He sounded stung, and Cat closed her eyes and tried again. "You know it's beautiful, but I didn't feel at home. It's all too much."

"It's just an apartment."

"Like you're just a man?" She laughed softly at the incomprehension in his voice. "You're Rafe Carlisle."

"So?"

Her eyes drifted open when she shook her head. "Do you really think you're no big deal?"

"To you I should be a big deal. I'm your husband."

"Well, there's a problem right there. I have trouble thinking of you as that. There's so much I still don't know about you."

"Then learn me," he rasped. Eyes sparking with what looked like irritation, he took her hand and put it on him, traced it over the hard sculpted muscles of his chest, rested it against the heavy thud of his heart until his heat seeped into her skin and chased through her blood.

Her husband. A mystery, a heartbreaker, a very big deal.

Cat shook her head.

"What?" he growled, leaning closer again, driving the worrying impact of that thought from her mind with the intensity of his expression. She lifted her other hand and traced the sculpted line of his jaw, his cheekbone and the brooding fullness of his mouth. Then she stretched up on her toes and kissed him with all she had to offer in her heart, while her fingers spread over his skin and learned the thick steady beat of his heart.

Her big-deal husband would break her heart when he left. She did not have enough to keep his attention here in the outback and she could not live in his city. He would leave and she would regret, but for now—this time and maybe again tomorrow, maybe a few more weekends—she would take what he had to give.

And she would give back in equal measure.

Easing back from that rich, earthy soul kiss, she touched his lips and asked, "Will you take my jeans off now?"

The corner of his mouth lifted under her fingers. "Are you asking nicely?"

Eyes linked with his, she slipped her other hand down his sleek wet hide until it closed around his sleek wet erection. "Is that nice enough?"

He licked at her bottom lip. "Did you say please?"

She squeezed until he groaned and pushed more fully into her hand. "Pretty please," she said sweetly. "With sugar on top."

He took her jeans off then, although it wasn't an easy task. The wet denim might well have shrunk already. It stuck to her skin and he kept dipping in to lick at each new exposed portion of her body. To nuzzle her thighs with the bristly texture of afternoon whiskers. To pump a new dose of body wash onto his hands and smooth it over her bottom and the backs of her legs.

By the time she kicked the weight of sodden denim aside she was breathing heavily and an inch away from begging. He rose in one smooth movement, and she saw the ripe color of arousal along his cheekbones and in his lust-dark eyes. They locked on hers, and his nostrils flared as she breathed one word.

"Yes."

His hands on her hips lifted her, a long cool slide against the wet tiles and she wrapped her arms around his neck and her legs around his hips. She felt him, hard and hot between her legs and felt a swell of need, unbearably intense.

"Take," she whispered against his mouth, "whatever you want."

His hands cupped her buttocks, held her there wide and open as he plunged, one full thrust of his hips that slid her hard against the tiles and drove the air from her lungs and filled her with heat and sensation and emotion so big it burst from her lips in a wild primal cry. But her eyes remained locked with his, linked in a supercharged arc of connection, lost in the sensual thrall of their sea-green intensity and the awed revelation that he felt the same magnitude, the same power, the same intensity.

He didn't need to touch her anywhere else, didn't need to do anything except drive her with the primitive rhythm of his body and look at her in exactly that way and whisper her name until she came apart in a swell of sensation that rose and rippled and peaked, only to come again as he drove deeper and faster and spilled himself in a spasm that resounded over and over and over in her blood.

She felt the slump of her boneless weight against the slick tiles and muttered something about letting her fall, and his grip on her hips tightened. "I won't let you fall, baby."

"I won't feel a thing if you do."

His laugh was a rasp of sound, and she smiled along with it, feeling marvelous and spent and impossibly invigorated all at once. Then his laughter exploded into a raw curse and rush of movement as he tried to evade the water that beat down on his back.

In the shelter of his body, Cat started to laugh. "I guess the hot water ran out," she gasped between chuckles.

He went very still. "So, my wife thinks that's funny."

"In a laughing *with you* kind of way."

"Huh." His eyes narrowed and gleamed dangerously. "They say marriage is about sharing…"

And she had barely enough time to yelp before he redirected the showerhead and a stream of cold water onto her.

* * *

Rafe turned off the water and warmed his wife's cool skin with a thorough toweling before he carried her from the bathroom.

"Where are you taking me?" she asked when he kept walking past the guest-room bed.

"Your bed." He stopped and looked into her face. "Did you expect I would want my own room?"

"No," she said without hesitation. "But I've been thinking about you in this bed."

"Have you, now."

"Ever since the night of your accident. When I undressed you."

"I will let you do that again one day." He started down the hallway. "Except, this time I'll be conscious."

She smiled and Rafe felt something stir through him and then settle rich and warm in his chest. Contentment. Satisfaction. And a major dose of sexual relief. A man should not have to wait five days to make love to his wife again. Not in the first week of his marriage.

"How many other places have you fantasized about having me?" he asked as he carted her into her bedroom.

"Besides in the guest-room shower?"

A bark of laughter escaped his throat as he sat on the bed and rolled with her until he had her positioned exactly where he wanted. Stretched out, with him on top. "So, Mrs. Carlisle. Did the reality live up to the fantasy?"

"In my fantasy I got to soap you. All over."

"Is that a complaint?"

"More an observation."

"Anything else you observed?"

Mischief gleamed green in her eyes. "My fantasies tend to be low on talking, big on action."

"My action not big enough for you?"

She wiggled her hips and then blinked slowly. "Already?"

"Just adapting to the concept of a long-distance relationship."

Something shifted in her eyes, a touch serious, a tad wary, and Rafe thought how easily he could chase that suspicion away. To sink down into a kiss and then into her body. But no matter what his friend downstairs might be signaling, he had taken the edge off his sexual hunger, and the mental side craved some loving, too.

He rolled onto his side, drawing her with him until they lay facing each other. He knew his expression had turned serious, knew because the wariness in her eyes had deepened. "I assume that's what you want," he said slowly. "Me flying out here on weekends and whenever else I can manage a night away."

"You'd do that?"

"I'll have to put some serious work in on your airstrip so I can land the Citation…but, yes."

Alarm widened her eyes. "You'd fly out here in a jet? Don't you need a—"

"Hey, I was joking." He leaned forward and kissed her. "But only about the jet."

That didn't erase the sharp notes of whatever worried her eyes. She stared at him, intent and silent for several seconds before she asked, "Why me?"

He knew what she meant: Why had he chosen her? He couldn't believe he hadn't told her, at least several times, but he could stretch himself to tell her again. "Originally? Because I liked you right off the bat and I knew you'd make a good mother."

"How can you say that?" A frown pleated her brow. "I'm used to being on my own. I don't mix with families. I don't have any experience with babies."

"Yeah, but the way you looked after me when I was concussed—that's the kind of care a mother should show. And then I saw you with those puppies." He shrugged. "I could picture you with a baby."

The fractiousness in her eyes settled, darkened, as if it turned inward. As if imagining that same picture.

Rafe realized then how quickly, how easily he'd grown used to the notion of a baby—*his* baby—when that thought had terrified the bejesus out of him two weeks ago. Who would have predicted it? An introspective smile played over his lips. "It's a great picture, isn't it?"

She nodded and attempted to return his smile. Hers wobbled a little at the edges. "I hope you're right about the mother call."

"How old were you when your mother died?" he asked, guessing at the cause of her concern.

"Four," she said softly. "I don't even remember her."

Sorry didn't cover something like that so he simply stroked a hand down her arm. "When did the wicked stepmother come into the picture?"

Her lips twitched. "I was twelve."

"And she made your life an instant misery."

"No, I was over-the-moon excited at first. A new mother who was beautiful and sophisticated and who brought me amazing gifts. Plus I was getting two sisters. Life was going to be perfect!"

The quiet shadow of sadness in her voice twisted Rafe's gut. He leaned forward and brushed a soft kiss to her lips, and another and another until he'd chased that unhappy curve away. "What dastardly things did she do?"

"Oh, nothing overt. She didn't make me scrub floors and chop firewood or anything. She just made me feel…less. Like no matter what I did I could never meet her standards. Then she started undermining my relationship with Dad. She even convinced him to send me to boarding school."

"Isn't that necessary?" he asked carefully. "Given your isolation?"

"Maybe, but I hated it from day one. I hated being away from home. I missed my dad and my animals like crazy."

She was silent a long while, but Rafe waited, knowing there was more. Knowing, instinctively, that this was crucial to understanding her and why she wouldn't spend time in the city.

"I was away at school when my father died. He was out mustering and he came off his bike. He broke his back and...other stuff." Her hand fluttered under his, her breath shuddered and hitched and pierced somewhere deep in his chest. "He was alive for close to twenty-four hours but no one found him. He died out there, alone."

"I'm sorry, baby" didn't even come close, but he said it anyway. He said it and he wrapped her in his arms and wished he could absorb all her hurt into his own body. Wished he could say that being there wouldn't have made any difference for her father but he didn't know that. He did know it would have made a hell of a difference to Catriona.

"Tell me about him."

"My dad? Oh, he was tall. Dark."

"And handsome?"

"*Rugged* I think is the right word." Wry and sad, her smile reached in and grabbed him where he lived. "He was built like a rugby second-rower, which was handy since that's the position he played."

"Lucky."

"He had a wicked sense of humor and a laugh that rolled up from his belly. I swear nobody could resist Dad's laugh."

"Sounds like you got a gem."

"Yeah, I did. What about you?" she asked after a beat.

"I got lucky when my mother married Charles Carlisle."

She watched him solemnly for a moment. "Have you ever met your birth father?"

"Once." Rafe played a long tress of her hair through his fingers. Then he shrugged. "I wish I hadn't bothered."

"Why's that?"

"He wasn't worth knowing."

The tenor of her expression changed, a subtle shift in the way she eyed him. Unease swirled in his belly because he knew he'd revealed more than he intended in that one flat statement. Knew that he had to divert her attention before she honed in on the one area of his life he didn't intend sharing.

He propped himself on an elbow and trailed a hand down her body, throat to navel in a drift of knuckles and warm velvet heat. "So, Mrs. Carlisle—"

"Are you trying to distract me?"

"No, I'm trying to keep on subject."

Her eyes narrowed. "Which subject would that be?"

"You asked why I thought you'd make a good mother. I hadn't finished answering." Curiosity flared in her eyes, then heat as he caressed the curve of her belly. "I knew you came from good stock. Strong character, sharp brain, smart mouth." Pausing for effect, he spanned her pelvis with his hand. "Good child-bearing hips."

Naturally she growled and swatted him.

Naturally he wrestled her to her back and pinned her to the bed with the weight of his body.

Naturally he kissed the fire from her lips and looked deep into her eyes and told her he was joking, that mostly he just enjoyed her better than any woman he'd ever met. In and out of bed. And then he let her roll him onto his back so he could enjoy the weight of her body and her eyes smiling into his and then not smiling at all as she took him inside her and consumed him with her heat.

Thirteen

Cat managed to keep him in her bed long enough that the Friday night show became a moot point. But she didn't forget how he'd distracted her from asking more about his birth father, or how much she had revealed in comparison. Over the next two days she tried to entice more from him, but he had a way of deflecting the conversation if he didn't like the topic, and he did so with such finesse that Cat didn't know she'd been stonewalled until afterward. Usually after a couple of orgasms and a nap to recover.

All weekend they worked together, sometimes in surprising harmony, but more often than not arguing about the most efficient method. Rafe might be good at giving, but he was not so good at giving in or at taking orders. He excelled, she discovered, at delegation and negotiation and cutting deals.

He excelled, too, at making her laugh and snarl within the same minute. At keeping her mind entertained and her tongue sharp and her body sated. Constantly she fought the notion that she was getting too used to his company and too comfortable in his company, with him wearing jeans and boots and working alongside her.

Or wearing nothing at all and working alongside, on top of or beneath her.

This time there'd been some of all three, and now Cat lay sprawled beside him in the Sunday twilight quiet. Spent and satisfied but also shadowed in sadness because early in the morning he was returning to Sydney. Back to his job and his apartment and the life she felt no more ready to be a part of than five days earlier.

He'd asked, several times. And she'd tried to explain that she didn't like the person she became in the city. Awkward and ill-at-ease and out of her element. She didn't like spending time there. She didn't want to damage what they'd forged this weekend, either.

Now, on the cooling sheets of her bed, she sensed him watching her again, and she didn't have to ask what he was thinking. "Leave it," she said, before he opened his mouth. "I won't change my mind."

"You said that about Vegas...."

"And look where that got me!"

Her debt paid off, a future for Corroboree, a possibility of family.

Feeling incredibly lucky and humbled and thankful, she turned her head to look at him. To quietly say, "Thank you."

He didn't smile and say, "My pleasure," as she'd anticipated. He didn't say anything for a long, solemn second. "How about you thank me by coming to Kameruka Downs next weekend."

Not the first time he'd broached the subject of taking her to meet his mother, either. She shook her head against the pillow. "No. Not yet."

"You're being stubborn."

"No, I'm being practical. I have responsibilities here. My animals—"

"The Porters looked after them while you were in America. Is there any reason they can't do that again?"

"I can't ask them every weekend."

"I'm not asking—"

"Please, Rafe," she cut in, quiet, intense. "Not yet."

For several strong, hard beats of her heart she didn't think he would let it go. He had that look in his eyes she didn't trust. That intentness and purpose that always set her on edge. But then he rolled onto his back and stared at the ceiling. "I'll come back here, then."

The tight breathlessness in Cat's chest eased. He was coming back. Another weekend, another chance to forge his indelible impression in her home and in her life. In her heart, too, but she was stoically trying to ignore that. "I hope you will."

"Why don't we invite your neighbors over," he asked after another short pause.

"Now?" she asked, rising on her elbow. Indicating their nakedness with an arched eyebrow.

"Next weekend."

"I gather you mean Bob and Jennifer Porter." She eyed him a moment, trying to work out his angle. Suspicious of this seemingly random idea coming hot on the heels of his latest invitation to spend a weekend away. "Are you thinking of using them to persuade me I'm not needed here? Because—"

"I'm thinking they're your closest neighbors and old family friends and you might like to introduce them to your husband."

Taken aback by his tone and the matching snap to his eyes, Cat blinked.

"Unless there's some reason you don't want to," he added.

"What would that be?"

"You tell me. You don't have a problem with having me here, putting me to work, having me in your bed…but you don't want to go anywhere with me. You don't want to meet my family or me to meet your neighbors. I'm starting to wonder if you don't want to be seen with me."

"Don't be ridiculous!"

"Am I?" He asked, low and dangerous. "Who have you told about our marriage, Catriona?"

Her silence was telling.

"Not even your stepmother? You told me last week you'd love to wipe the floor with her patronizing attitude. Aren't I a big enough prize?"

"Is that how you see yourself?" she countered. "Is that how you'd like me to introduce you to my neighbors next weekend? Jen and Bob, meet Rafe Carlisle, my prize husband. I won him on the roulette wheel in Vegas!"

He glared at her a long moment, then he shook his head and expelled a low oath. "I would like you to introduce me as your husband. That's all."

"I can do that," she said softly, relenting. "Saturday night?"

"Saturday night is good."

As always, the heat of their exchange shifted to another kind of heat, and he made love to her with an edgy intensity that set her pulse hammering and her blood roaring. And when he held her on the brink, fire burned in his gaze as he insisted on hearing his name on her lips.

Cat didn't think about that conversation again until after he'd gone. Around midmorning on Monday she was drawing up a working budget—arguably the world's most boring task—when she recalled Milla's words that day on his terrace.

He's a better man than he lets on, even to himself.

Unsettled, she rocked back from her computer spreadsheet and onto her feet. She knew she'd underestimated him from the start, dismissing him as lightweight and a charming diversion. That seemed to come so easily to him—he played on it, she knew—yet there were so many other layers to the man.

Depth and capability and intelligence that he liked to bury beneath the sexy, playboy charm.

Now she wondered why…and Milla's comment and that Sunday evening conversation drifted through her consciousness.

Surely he couldn't have any kind of inferiority thing. Not Rafe Carlisle. Surely he didn't believe that she'd kept their marriage from her friends and distant family because *he* was lacking. That was laughable in an ironic way, seeing as she'd been thinking the exact opposite.

That *she* might be seen as deficient by *his* family and friends.

She knew she lacked nothing here in her environment, in the life she'd chosen as a child riding at her father's side. Here she was herself, she was happy, and that was that. If she fell pregnant, she would have an added link with his family, a bond beyond her marriage.

Then she would travel to Kameruka Downs and meet his mother. Then he could take her to a fancy restaurant to lunch with his brothers, but not before. It would be hard enough saying goodbye to Rafe when he decided to end their marriage.

She did not want to lose her heart to his family, as well.

Cat hated to admit it—even to herself—but all week she'd been like a kid waiting for Christmas. She had enough work to fill her days. She had his phone calls to look forward to each night. It shouldn't have taken so long for Friday to come around. And when it did and she arrived home to a message saying he wouldn't be arriving until Saturday, she should not have felt such a dismal sense of letdown.

It's okay, Cat told herself, since she wasn't a kid waiting for Christmas. She was an adult. Independent and capable of dealing with the first hiccup in their long-distance marriage. He, too, had responsibilities.

Saturday morning she'd intended to wait for Rafe before

starting work, but the early arrival of her period had her wired tight and sharp as a newly strained barb. She couldn't sit around wringing her hands in disappointment because she hadn't fallen pregnant the first time. Now, there was no reason not to yard the cows herself.

Mustering gave her some time to think and to decide she didn't like her happiness hanging on his arrival or nonarrival. Perhaps she should reevaluate their relationship. Perhaps the long distance thing would never work.

And perhaps she shouldn't make any decisions on a day when she felt so funky and out of sorts. Or while working with large, unpredictable animals, she added, when a cow balked suddenly almost knocking the gate from her hands.

She paid more attention then, as she prepared to start drafting off the dry cows. The day was warm already, the air thick with dust churned by racing hooves. She ducked through the railed fence and was unlatching the gate at the end of the draft when she thought she heard the buzz of a plane overhead. Even as she tipped back her hat to scan the sky she called herself silly. The airstrip hadn't been graded. He would fly to the Samuelses' again.

Swinging back, she saw the danger a millisecond too late. A cow hit the gate she held, knocking it from her grip and driving it into her chest. Before she could regain her balance, the whole yard sniffed the open gate and charged full tilt for freedom.

This time the iron bar caught her on the side of the head and she went down for the count.

Rafe had a bad feeling gnawing at him all the way from Sydney. It made him fly cautiously for a change, but once on the ground and behind the wheel of his borrowed vehicle he nearly flew the ten miles to Corroboree. He barely slowed for the cattle grids or the sharp turn by the house. He could see the dust cloud of activity at the cattle yards a mile farther on that confirmed his gut feeling was spot-on.

He'd told her not to start without him. She'd argued that she'd been working cattle on her own since her teens. He pointed out that since he had a vested interest, he'd prefer she didn't do such work on her own again. Not when she could be pregnant.

"And of course you have to do it your way," he ground out as he wheeled to a halt beside the yards.

His hot anger morphed to cold fear the second he slammed the door on the utility. The cattle wheeled around the yards in obvious agitation stirring up a choking cloud of dust, but even through that he should have been able to pick out Cat's figure.

He couldn't. Yet her bike was here. He took the fence at a run, climbing two rails at a time and feeling his heart lurch in his chest when he saw her from the top. Crouched in the corner of the yard, her dog at her feet.

He called her name as he hit the ground, but the croaky sound was swallowed up in the bellowing chaos of the startled herd. *She's all right, she's conscious, she's trying to get to her feet, she's all right,* chanted through his mind as he pushed through the next fence and finally she looked up, her face pale beneath a coating of dust, a smile trembling on her lips.

Her legs started to wobble, and before he could get there she started to sink to the ground. Rafe hunkered down with her, his own limbs felt wonky with fear and shock and relief because at least she was conscious.

"It's okay, baby," he told her. "I'm here now."

Her attempt at a smile was wan. "There's two of you."

"That's a good thing, surely."

"Ish it?" There was a definite slur to her speech. "'Nough trouble handling one…"

Her voice trailed off as she slumped into unconsciousness and Rafe swore silently as he bent to scoop her up.

"You just need more practice."

* * *

Cat couldn't remember anything about the accident or getting to the hospital. Dimly she recalled an altercation over her admission and the objections swirling in her dizzy brain because she didn't want to be hospitalized. She remembered being blindsided by the pain of her head injury and her broken ribs, and the sharp note in Rafe's voice as he demanded a doctor's attention.

Sometime later she'd drifted into consciousness and he was there, sitting beside her bed, holding her hand and murmuring something she couldn't catch through the blur of pain medication. She'd floated back to sleep with a smile on her lips and in her heart, but when she woke again the chair was empty. Perhaps it was the drugs, but that small vignette of the big picture had seemed profoundly significant. He'd been there, looking out for her, making her smile, easing her loneliness, and then he was gone.

On Monday, when she opened her eyes and found him smiling down at her, the sweet ache of joy was almost unbearable. She could have put that down to her injuries—her chest hurt like the devil—but deep inside she acknowledged the inevitable. She wanted the glorious impossibility of Rafe Carlisle's smile whenever she opened her eyes. She wanted him as her real husband, at her side, forever.

In that instant she knew that nothing less than his love would do.

"Nice shiner," he drawled, parking himself on the edge of her mattress. But the kiss he pressed to her lips was tender, the depths of his eyes dark with concern.

"You're here."

"Did you think I'd leave you? All beaten up? In this place?"

"I thought…" Her frown hurt like the blazes, but not as much as the leap of her heart against her bruised and broken ribs. "I thought, maybe, you would need to be at work today."

"I needed to be here today." He lifted her hand and held it against his face for a second. "How are you feeling?"

"Like I was trampled by a herd of beasts."

The low note of his laughter did glorious things to her aching body. So did the brush of his fingers against her cheek. "I brought you some flowers and fruit."

"Thank you."

"And this."

"This" turned out to be diamonds. A diamond necklace, to be precise. Cat blinked in shock. Then—she couldn't help herself—she laughed. Flowers and fruit and, as an aside, diamonds. That was so over-the-top. So Rafe.

And so not her.

The laughter, the warmth, her delight in his presence suddenly turned brittle. She stared at the dazzling stones without touching them. "Where on earth did you get that?"

"In Vegas."

"It's…" *The same as those clothes. Beautiful, expensive, impractical.*

"You don't like it?" With a casual-looking shrug, he snapped the lid of the box shut and tossed it on the bedside table. "No matter."

But it did matter. In all kinds of ways. It mattered that he'd spent all that money on her…and that he didn't seem to care whether she liked the gift or not. Easy come, easy go. He could afford to buy a necklace like that with his lunch money. He was Rafe Carlisle.

It mattered even more over the next few days as he breezed in and out of the hospital, coloring the spare hospital room with his beauty, dazzling the nursing staff with his sexy grin, and entertaining her with his company, with covert kisses, and with news from Corroboree.

At first his interest and involvement in her station pleased her no end. They *did* have common ground. They just might have grounds for a relationship that worked in places other than in bed. Then she learned of the changes he was making, the money he was spending, all communicated in the same negligent tone as he'd delivered the diamonds.

I bought you a new Landcruiser. I've ordered a new hot water system. You need a better kitchen.

It mattered that he was infiltrating her life, her home, her business. Corroboree was *hers,* and she needed to keep control of that one last bastion. Her last remaining link with her parents; her strength; her confidence.

It mattered that when she attempted to explain this to Rafe, he shrugged it off in a way that grated all over nerves stretched taut by her enforced inactivity. "I want to do this for you, baby. I can afford it. Indulge me." Then he'd distracted her with wicked suggestions of how he'd like to indulge her in the new spa bath he'd ordered.

Today it had to end. Everything…including her hospital stay, which she was sure had stretched longer than necessary due to Rafe's influence. She was itching to get back home, to take over her life, but Rafe threw her planned speech right off balance by arriving on the heels of the breakfast cart—at least three hours before official visiting hours—dressed in a suit.

"I'm on my way to the airport," he told her after a soul-stirring kiss. "Board meeting I can't miss."

While she was recovering from his unexpected arrival, from the aftershocks of his kiss, he nabbed a piece of toast from her plate.

"Had to leave too early for breakfast," he said around his first bite. Then, "I saw your doctor outside. He says you'll be all right to go home tomorrow. I'll—"

"Today."

Rafe stopped chewing.

"I'm all right to go home today, if anyone would care to consult with me."

"Look, baby—"

"Oh, no. Don't even start with that."

"What?" he asked, genuinely puzzled.

"'Look, baby. Don't worry, baby. I'm handling everything, baby.'" Apparently, she was mocking his tone, although not very well. She shook her head and continued in her own voice. "I tried to explain this yesterday, and I'm going to try again now. I don't want you handling everything. I want to worry about my business, about my life."

"Okay."

"Okay?"

Alerted by her sharp inflection, by the glint of temper in her eyes, Rafe put down the remains of the toast and brushed the crumbs from his fingers. "Is there something specific I've done to upset you?"

"Everything you've done without asking first upsets me! The new vehicle, the stove, the spa you tossed into the equation."

"They're just things, Catriona. To make your life easier."

"They're things I didn't ask for, things I don't want." Her brows drew together in an uncompromising line. "None of this was part of our deal, Rafe."

"Can't I buy—"

"No. Don't you see? You're buying me all these *things* because you can afford to fling money around, and I have nothing to give back!"

One side of him wanted to say straight out that she didn't need to give anything back but herself, while the other balked at her attitude. At what sounded very much like a rejection of all he'd done for her and his reason for doing so. "You know why I married you, Catriona. I've told you more than once. Can't you accept that I don't need any more from you?"

Something shifted in her expression, almost as if she was gathering herself, preparing herself. "I'm not pregnant."

Rafe stared back at her. She thought he only wanted a baby? Hell, he—

"I don't know why I expected I would be. I just…"

Her voice trailed off, one hand lifted and then dropped to the blanket in a gesture of futility. Without thinking he reached for her—for that hand—but she pulled herself upright, warning him away with her body language and her eyes.

Rafe felt that rejection like a slap. He felt his own gaze narrow and instead of asking if she felt the same kick of disappointment as he did, instead of reassuring her that they could try again next month and the one after that if she wanted, he asked, "How long have you known?"

"Since Saturday."

Four days. At least six separate hospital visits, six opportunities to share the news. "And you didn't think I would want to know before now?"

"It doesn't make any difference," she said. "This isn't something you can go out and buy."

"Is that what you think I would want to do?"

"You bought me to have your baby."

He couldn't dispute that, didn't want to debate it. But he needed to get one thing straight… "That might be how we started out, but a lot has changed in the last two weeks."

"Has it?" she asked after a beat, and the quiet question rocked him back on his heels. Nothing had changed for her, he realized. Nothing.

"You only wanted the money to secure Corroboree? That's the only reason you married me?"

Her gaze met his, honest and unflinching. "I wanted the baby, too."

But not him. Never him.

Oddly the knowledge didn't spark heat or frustration or denial. Instead it turned him cold and numb some place deep inside. Frozen with an understanding that had been too slow coming. She didn't want him buying her things because she didn't want him. He'd made no impression on her heart, so everything he'd done—the things she knew, the ones she'd yet to discover—meant nothing to her except as an affront to her independence.

The very thing that had drawn him to her in the first place. How ironic.

"Tell me one thing, Catriona," he said slowly, coolly. "If

you'd had you choice of a father for this baby, would I have even figured in your selection process?"

For a second her eyes widened, raw with an emotion he couldn't identify, and then she looked away. And that telling silence cut through his numbness, sliced all the way to his soul.

As he'd expected, as he'd feared—he wasn't the man she would have chosen. He wasn't a man she could ever love.

"Rafe, I'm sorry."

And that was the last thing he needed. Her pity, an apology, some tepid justification. "Hey, babe," he drawled, as if it didn't matter a damn to him. "There's no need for you to be sorry. You've got your property back and a few extras into the bargain. Why should you be sorry?"

"I thought you needed this baby."

He gave a shrug. "There's time to try again."

A pulse beat hard in her throat as she slowly shook her head. "I don't think so, Rafe. I think…I think I need some time alone to reconsider."

"Take all the time you want, Catriona. I won't come chasing you again. If you ever change your mind, you know where to find me."

Fourteen

When the hospital discharged her later that day, Bob Porter was waiting to take her home. Bob didn't volunteer how he came to be there and Cat's pride didn't let her ask. She must have nodded off as soon as they hit the road because she woke at home with Bob shaking her arm, and she didn't recall anything of the trip.

Still groggy, she stumbled inside and pulled up short when she found his wife inside. Cleaning.

"You didn't have to do this," Cat said.

"Just getting used to the place."

Cat frowned. Perhaps the rap on the head had affected her more than she'd thought.

The other woman smiled secretly. "He said it would be a nice surprise."

A tight feeling gathered in the center of her chest, like a knot being tugged hard from either side. "He?"

"He, your husband." Jennifer winked conspiratorially. "He headhunted us, you know."

"Headhunted?" Cat's voice sounded as weak and thready as her knees. She needed to sit down. She did. And Jennifer looked concerned. "Are you all right, love?"

"I will be once you stop dragging out the suspense. What are you talking about, Jen?"

"Our new jobs. Bob's your stationhand. I'm the house-keeper. We weren't supposed to start for a couple more weeks, but Gordon didn't take the news of us leaving well. He told us not to bother working our notice. We were going to take a holiday but then your Rafe rang and told us about your accident…. We thought it might be nice to start straight away."

"I'm all right, Jen. Really. I don't need any house help."

Jen ignored that. "Can I make you a cuppa?"

Cat nodded. She needed to sit and digest this a minute. Work through how this had happened…and what she was going to do about it. The knot in her chest tightened several more notches as she thought about that argument in the hospital. The coldness in Rafe's eyes before he walked from the room.

"When did Rafe employ you?" she asked, turning toward the kitchen where Jen was setting down their cups.

"He rang last week. Tuesday—no, it was Monday night. He made us an offer and we asked for some time to think it over."

Last week? And she'd known nothing about it… "Why didn't you ask me what I thought about this?"

"Rafe said he wanted to tell you himself." Jen smiled. "I told him it was the kind of present you would appreciate. You not being one for jewelry and the like."

"What did he say to that?" Cat's throat felt tight, her voice husky with the certainty she'd made the biggest blunder of her life. That she'd done Rafe a serious disservice.

"He said he was working that out. And I have to agree, given his other surprise."

A peach orchard.

Cat's heart stalled when Jen spilled that news, and restarted with a thick, slow beat that ached through her body. He'd remembered what she'd told him in Vegas about loving the scent of freshly picked peaches. As soon as Bob rang back accepting the job, Rafe had talked to him about how and when and where to put the new trees.

All she'd wanted was some sign that he cared, that he might even love her, and now she had it—a peach orchard, the perfect sign—and it was too late. She'd sent him away. She'd let him believe there was nothing between them, that she wanted nothing between them.

If he didn't care, why would he have chosen something this personal? This special?

If he didn't care, why would he have told her where to find him if she reconsidered? Wouldn't he have simply told her to forget it? To forget him?

Her heart beat so hard it echoed in her ears, drumming with the clear certainty of what she had to do. She didn't want to give up. She didn't want to be lonely anymore. She didn't need to reconsider when the truth beat so strongly in her heart.

Rafe was operating on autopilot. Shaking hands. Dispensing small talk. Smiling and sipping the sponsor's champagne at yet another charity event and all the while thinking, *How long until I can get the hell out of here? Until I can go somewhere to snap and snarl the way my gut and my heart and my head have been doing all night long. All week long.*

Ever since Catriona convinced him he was wasting his time. That he wasn't the kind of man she would ever choose.

He didn't blame her. This whole scheme had been flawed from the start. He'd been too clever, thinking he wanted an independent wife who made no demands upon his heart or his lifestyle.

That's what he'd wanted; that's what he'd got. How could he complain?

Surreptitiously he checked his watch again. Eight o'clock.

He'd intended staying another hour, but in his current mood it was wiser to cut and run. Before he snarled at someone important and cost the hotel a big corporate client.

He made his excuses to the head of the charity committee, promised her a donation that wiped the moue of disappointment off her lips and was in a taxi heading home before she stopped gushing her thanks.

In the last week there'd been a lot he didn't like about his apartment—specifically, being alone in it—but one thing he appreciated right now was its location so close to the city. He was walking through the lobby of his building five minutes later. Pressing the elevator button. Rocking on his heels and wondering what the hell better things he had to do upstairs tonight. Alone.

Ah, hell, at least he could smash a glass if he felt like it. Snarl at Tolstoy. Play some tragic opera at full volume and wallow in his misery.

The elevator dinged. Not the one he faced but the one at his back. He turned on his heel as the doors opened and the woman inside looked up and right in to his eyes.

Her coral-painted lips mouthed one word. His name. But she didn't move, and Rafe found himself frozen in place, stunned, wondering if his imagination had conjured her up.

A vision in white satin sent to taunt his lonely night.

Then the elevator doors slid noiselessly shut and propelled him into motion. He dived for the button just as the doors reopened. He met her on her way out and turned her back inside. Closed the doors.

"What are you doing here?" She sounded as incredulous as he felt. Looked even more beautiful up close. And she was real.

"I live here." He met her eyes. Cool. Polite. "You?"

"I…know someone who lives here."

"You were visiting?"

"I came to visit." She lifted her chin a little, and he saw the nervous tick of the pulse in her throat. Watched the nervous flick of her tongue as she moistened her lips. "To stay, actually. But he wasn't home."

Rafe felt something flutter back to life deep inside. "Weren't you going to stick around and wait for this…someone…to come home?"

"I thought about that," she said gravely. "I was going to climb into his bed and wait."

"A sound plan."

"But we have some problems to iron out, and they never seem to be a problem in bed. Out of bed…that's what we need to work on."

He nodded. And he let his eyes drift over her dress. The one he'd opened in that box in Vegas. It looked even better on her body, and the diamonds at her throat were the perfect foil. Slowly his gaze rose to meet hers. "So you decided to go out somewhere?"

"I wasn't sure what to do. My husband didn't know I was coming to town, you see—"

"This man's your husband?"

"He is." Despite her nerves, despite the wild uncertainty of her heartbeat, Cat stood tall and sure. This was her one chance to let him see what he meant to her. "He is my husband who I sent away because I didn't understand how much he had given me or how well he knew me."

"And now you do?"

"Yes, and I want to tell him so. Except I didn't know where he was or how long he would be. So I asked his neighbor and she told me he'd gone to this charity party, an important one for his work, and I decided to go, too. To talk to him."

"About those problems you mentioned before…?"

"That's right." She moistened her lips again, but her eyes never left his. "I have this fear, you see, about getting dressed up like this and going to a fancy party where I'll be looked over and judged by people such as my husband's family and friends and business colleagues. Important people I want to make an impression with, but there's this fear I'll be found wanting."

"Sounds as if you were about to face up to this fear."

"I was. For him." She sucked in a breath that hitched a little before continuing. "Then there's my stubbornness. I'm used to doing things my own way."

"Independence isn't all bad."

"I'm starting to think I overrated it. That it might be nice to have a partner to share life with. Not part-time, and maybe full-time won't be possible, but more of the time."

Rafe felt his nostrils flare. Felt that flutter of hope grow wings that beat hard and fast. "Sounds as if you're working on that problem, too."

"I think so. But there's another one." Nerves swam in her eyes and he had to steel himself to stay put. To let her get all the way through whatever she'd come here to say before he gave in to the need to hold her. "The last time I saw my husband, he asked if I would have chosen him."

"Perhaps he didn't think he had enough to offer."

Her head lifted a little. Some kind of recognition or acknowledgment flared in her eyes. "He couldn't possibly think that. He's the most amazing man I've ever met. Oh, he's passably handsome and he has some charm, but that's by the by." Slowly she took a step toward him. "The thing I failed to see was how well he knew me. I kept focusing on the little things." Another step. "He didn't know what I liked to eat. I didn't know his address. He didn't know that white satin evening dresses have limited wear out west." One more step and she stopped right in front of him. Her voice dropped to a new, low resonance, in perfect harmony with Rafe's pulse. "But he knew what was important. He gave me the most precious things. My family property. A chance to have a family again. The perfect staff. And then there's the peach orchard…"

The last came more slowly, on a slightly quizzical note that dampened Rafe's stampeding hope. "You don't like the idea?"

"An orchard is a lot of work."

His eyes narrowed in alarm. "What are you saying, Catriona?"

"I'm going to need someone to share the workload," she said solemnly. "And to share the peaches."

"That sounds like a long-term project."

"Like a marriage, I was thinking. It takes a lot of nurturing and a lot of love, but then you've got something to show for your devotion and something to leave to future generations."

"Are there going to be future generations?" he asked, heart beating strong and fast again.

"I hope so." Finally she lifted a hand and touched his face. Reaching out and letting him know she was willing to give, willing to take the first step, willing to meet him halfway. "I love you, Rafe Carlisle. I want to make those future generations with you."

"You would trust me with such an important long-term project?"

"I trust you with my heart, husband."

His heart responded, believing, trusting. "Then that is all I want from you. I love you, Catriona McConnell Carlisle. Will you marry me, again? In front of family and friends?"

"Yes." Smiling her love, she moved into his arms. "I will."

* * * * *

Look for Alex Carlisle's story,
THE RUTHLESS GROOM (#1691),
in November 2005
only from Silhouette Desire.

If you enjoyed what you just read,
then we've got an offer you can't resist!

Take 2 bestselling love stories FREE!

Plus get a FREE surprise gift!

SAGA

National bestselling author

Debra Webb

A decades-old secret threatens to bring down Chicago's elite Colby Agency in this brand-new, longer-length novel.

COLBY CONSPIRACY

While working to uncover the truth behind a murder linked to the agency, Daniel Marks and Emily Hastings find themselves trapped by the dangers of desire—knowing every move they make could be their last....

Available in October, wherever books are sold.

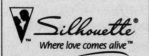

Where love comes alive™

Bonus Features include:

Author's Journal, Travel Tale and a Bonus Read.

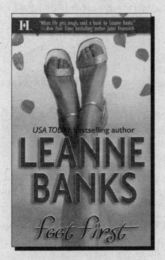

Silhouette®

Desire

COMING NEXT MONTH

#1681 THE HIGHEST BIDDER—Roxanne St. Claire
Dynasties: The Ashtons
A sexy millionaire bids on a most unlikely bachelorette and gets the surprise of his life.

#1682 DANGER BECOMES YOU—Annette Broadrick
The Crenshaws of Texas
Two strangers find themselves snowbound and looking for ways to stay warm, while staying out of danger.

#1683 ROUND-THE-CLOCK TEMPTATION—
Michele Celmer
Texas Cattleman's Club: The Secret Diary
This tough Texan bodyguard is offering his protection…day and night!

#1684 A SCANDALOUS MELODY—Linda Conrad
The Gypsy Inheritance
She'll do anything to keep her family's business…even become her enemy's mistress.

#1685 SECRET NIGHTS AT NINE OAKS—Amy J. Fetzer
When a wealthy recluse hides from the world, only one woman can save him from his self-imposed exile.

#1686 WHEN THE LIGHTS GO DOWN—Heidi Betts
Plain Jane gets a makeover and a lover who wants to turn their temporary tryst into a permanent arrangement.

SDCNM0905